DIVINE THEFT

Exposing the Hijacked Savior

How a Rebranded Faith Is Fueling
a Political Coup and Threatening Our Future

Hope's Journal of Kolob
An Identity Heist Companion

Lindsay McGuire

Table of Contents

Introduction

I am your guide on a journey to expose how a faith once claiming divine origins has become a political machine. Divine Theft lays bare three pivotal truths:

1. From its inception, the Church of Jesus Christ of Latter-day Saints, formerly known simply as Mormonism, has operated secretly as a corporate enterprise, using tax-exempt status to amass a global real estate and investment empire. Those billions of dollars in corporate dominance influences politics in an international scope.

2. Doctrinal shifts—such as the 1978 priesthood extension vote— reflect brand management rather than unchanging revelation, contradicting Hebrews 13:8 and Numbers 23:19.

3. True Christianity, rooted in the unchanging Christ of the Bible, rejects a "continuing revelation" that distorts truth for profit and influence greater than the Roman Cesar whom Christ did not mingle His might with or come to shape, for a post-apocalyptic purpose known only to those within the entity of the godmakers.

Together, we'll explore the clash between the pseudo-religion of the LDS hierarchy and the Savior of the New Covenant, reclaiming His name, His nature, and the hope of genuine faith.

Preface — Hope's Journal

I vividly recall the moment I realized the boundary between sacred sanctuary and corporate boardroom had vanished. It wasn't a dramatic event; rather, it was the slow drip of brown water from a farmhouse spigot, the taste of tea deemed sinful, and the quiet tally of billions hidden behind shell companies. My heart broke when I recognized how a faith that promised living water instead drained real lives.

In this Journal, we will:

- Uncover the corporate machinery—what my children call the *Temple-Spin-Doctor-Engine*—that repurposes sacred tithes into skyscrapers, ranches, and tech fortunes.
- Expose the brand-management votes and doctrinal U-turns that clash with the unchanging Christ of Scripture.
- Trace the human cost: mothers stripped of custody, children baptized in fear, and grandfathers who died fighting these lies.

This is not an academic exposé. It is a true memoir of betrayals cloaked in sacred names, with an adapted courtroom drama, and real battle hymns. You'll step into the shoes of a battered mother who fled motel rooms, navigated secret safe houses, and faced explosive bomb threats with other promises of death— all while holding her children under a divine banner that refused to be hijacked.

What Awaits You

1. Vivid, true-to-life scenes—from a midnight farmhouse rescue to a courtroom's decisive gavel.

2. Razor-sharp contrasts between corporate-driven "continuing revelation" in the Mormon or Latter Day Saint political and corporate rebranded "religious" fear-mongering organization built upon generations of heart-wrenching untruths versus the timeless Gospel of the unfiltered and truthfully translated Biblical Christian Messiah.

3. The beginning practical steps to reclaim your own banner of truth: identifying forces that bind you and finding the path to genuine freedom.

I've poured every ounce of sweat, tears, and legal filings into these pages. My hope is that you'll finish this book not just informed but armed—ready to protect the truth that anchors you and your family and preserves your future.

Let us begin the journey. The real Savior is waiting.

Hope Livingston – as Journaled and archived by Author Lindsay McGuire

For more personal encounters to heal from religious harm, or to grow intimately with the Creator, Triune God of the Christian Bible, find:

The Carpenter's Call `~ Identity Reclaimed
Journal and Book series by Lindsay McGuire

Chapter 1

Farmhouse Refuge

Rural East Coast Barrens, late June, 9:07 p.m.

Hope Livingston eased the midnight blue, quasar-speckled van onto the weed-choked verge. Her headlights illuminated an abandoned mailbox—its crooked post half-swallowed by blackberry vines. Just beyond, a gravel lane wound toward a two-story farmhouse painted the color of forgotten bone. She backed the van in tight next to the side gate, plates to the rear, and turned off the engine, listening intently: no trailing engine, no sudden crack echoing an explosive charge. Crickets thrummed on both sides of the narrow blacktop; humidity clung to her cheeks like damp gauze. Safe—for the moment.

Sebastian was still squinting to read from the SEC's 2023 disclosure on Ensign Peak. Hope's youngest children tumbled out but stayed close to their mother and each other, the buddy system in play, stiff from the three-hour drive south from the Dindy Motel. Emma (sixteen) rolled her shoulders and inhaled the scents of pine tar and honeysuckle, hoping to forget a lifetime of rejection and betrayal, beckoned by the upward-arching pines to take in the starlit sky above them. Leo (fifteen) rubbed a sleep crease from his cheek, trying to appear fearless in the face of terroristic promises of erasure to all he held dear. Sebastian (thirteen) put the papers in his pant pocket and clicked his multitool open and shut, scanning rooflines as if assessing structural load and monitoring the air in hyper-vigilance for any sign of the people he hoped his family had left behind. The twins, Matthew and Molly, followed, yawning and clutching one of the smoke-stained blankets their mother had packed after nine months at the Dinty Motel.

Anna (ten) held Sammy's five-year-old hand and whispered,

"We're really here."

Sammy whispered back, "Anna-Sis, can they erase us here, too?"

Sammy trembled partly with an angst too heavy for any child and partly from the cool relief after their long ride in the van, his little body shocked by the heat wave that hit them all like a wall as the door slid open to let the outside in, recalling Jemma and Fowley's speaker-phone promises—Anyone can just disappear...explosives...no trace, no witnesses—still echoed inside every heartbeat.

Hope stepped onto the porch. The boards flexed but held. She keyed the door, her heart fluttering at its hollow clap. A single bare bulb in the foyer revealed what the ARC church members had managed to cobble together in their Domestic Violence Safe House after their former tenants found a more permanent home. A queen mattress lay in the middle of the living room floor, three twins stacked against the wall, two thrift-store sofas parked under lasagna-pan windows, and a pine table big enough for a small revival. Nine ladder-back chairs stood around it like sentries.

Dinner awaited in a cooler—sandwiches labeled SILENT BLESSINGS— with love from Amy and Paul Gideon and family.

Silence meant safety; Hope's throat tightened with gratitude and grief.

"Beds!" Molly shouted, launching onto the queen. Springs groaned; Hope's fifth-youngest child bounced. Emma giggled—a quick, startled sound

Hope hadn't heard in months. Leo vaulted over the back of a faded floral sofa and sprawled with victorious abandon.

Hope's gratitude burned so bright it nearly blinded her to the missing pieces of herself—until Sebastian reported that the house was safe. Even the air thick with sticky heat filled every kitchen drawer and cabinet. No forks. No pans. Nothing. The farmhouse exhaled its war-worn emptiness.

"Mom, look!" Matthew twisted the century-old faucet. Water gurgled, then flowed the color of weak Earl Grey. He gasped, naively. "Is this real tea?!"

Molly's face blanched. "If we drink tea or coffee, the bishop said we go to Outer Darkness... What are our Eternal Consequences if we take our baths in tea?"

Hope's stomach knotted. She shut the tap, her palm recoiling, still tingling from the rusty droplets and from the prospect of eternal damnation looming over her and her youngest children. With a spirit of resolve that had become her ally, she forced steadiness into her voice.

"We'll find clear water. Promise." Hope's mind raced through memories of teachings, Bishopric interviews, testimonies, and sermons that made any tea or coffee hotter than imagined hell for other Christians. Tea was of course as sinful as street drugs or coffee, yet the quiet tally of over $30 Billion hidden in shell companies and stock holdings by the Modern day Presidencies went unmentioned from the pulpit of from General Conferences. To raise a question, to dare ask or seem to question brought eternal consequences, as those of us with a Temple Recommend, hell might seem welcome, as our fate is the promise of eternities confined to icy solitude in Outer Darkness. We're stricken from the Book of Life if we dare defy The Latter-Day Saint Word of Wisdom or question the Priesthood; stripped not just from the Lord's presence in the afterlife, but from any loved one's memory and shunned with sure sentence of floating alone in bitter darkness; for eternity.

From the van's rear hatch, Hope retrieved two flashlights she'd packed in Main with their camping supplies and tossed them to Leo and Sebastian. "Check for an outdoor spigot. Matthew, you insisted—go help your brothers."

They returned triumphant minutes later, hose in hand, announcing that the stream ran crystal—or at least appeared that way under moonlight. Hope rummaged through the laundry bags she'd folded at the motel coin-op that afternoon. Clean swimsuits, still smelling of lavender detergent, surfaced like treasures, along with some now-fraying but smoke-free, fresh towels.

Outside, the hose hissed to life. The first blast hit Anna square in the back; she shrieked, half in pain, half delight. Leo swung the nozzle heavenward, and cold water arced over the grass, raining down like liquid stardust.

Sebastian darted through, yelping "Incoming!" Sammy squealed "Waterfall!" until his voice cracked. Each icy droplet peeled away a layer of motel smoke and road sweat, rinsing it into the earth. Hope joined them last—fully clothed, arms raised—letting the chill bite her skin, false shame, and toxic guilt alike.

Laughter spilled across the yard, loud enough to make bullfrogs pause. Hope tasted salt—part hose water, part tears—and thanked her Savior for this mercy stream.

When shivering turned to chatter, she herded her family inside. Clean but thinner towels absorbed water and some part of their fear. Emma passed her oversized hoodie to Anna; Leo draped a Sixers T-shirt over Matthew like a poncho. On the queen mattress, the five youngest collapsed in a tangle. Emma and Leo pulled two twin mattresses to lay under the sagging ceiling upstairs and helped the youngest move the queen up the steep wooden staircase. Hope limped in stabbing pain throughout her torso and legs as she dragged the last twin mattress halfway down the attic floor, then thought better of it, dropping the mattress where it lay and hauling a scratchy wool blanket onto the floral sofa for her makeshift bed with the others downstairs.

Only then did quiet descend—punctuated surprisingly by cicadas, an owl's throaty question, and a distant freight whistle. Hope dialed Amy Gideon, her hand trembling.

"Amy," she whispered. "This dinner, this house—a Godsend. Thank you! But Amy—rusty water, no pans, no fan or air-conditioning. I thought this house would be, well, like Dad's—a safe place for the children and for me to collect ourselves while... I don't know."

Static, then Amy's warm hush: "Trust and obey, Hope—that's still the way forward. Tomorrow we'll fix the pipes, bring dishes, linens, maybe a fan. Let tonight be a first step."

Hope swallowed a sob. "That was a favorite verse that the Bishops and Sisters used, even outside the Temple... but it feels different coming from you."

"Different source and no hidden agenda," Amy said. "Sleep if you can. Pray to trust yourself again."

After the call ended, Hope leaned against the doorframe. Instinctively, she hummed the pioneer hymn drilled into her childhood: Put your shoulder to the wheel, push along... The melody felt both like a knife and a salve.

"Trust *MYSELF?*" Hope marveled at the audacity of the thought.

"Who am I? Just a WOMAN- no Priest, and not Saint-worthy," her thoughts trailed off.

Her phone buzzed: Sato Spine—Pre-op check-in, 7 days, 06:45 AM. Hope thumbed the screen dark. Above, floorboards creaked as the children shifted in sticky sleep. The air felt heavy, but for once her lungs accepted it.

Hope's Journal – 11:59 p.m.

Day 1—disasters avoided.

Brown water. No pots. Hose shower = laughter. Thank You?

Amy says trust & obey. Bishop said the same words, different tone. Sleepless but alive.

Will write more in the morning.

A floorboard above groaned; Leo's voice muttered, "I'm okay." Hope pressed a palm to the rough plaster, as if steadying the whole house.

Through the window, the hose dripped silver threads onto crabgrass. Crickets played a fragile lullaby. Hope inhaled pine and damp dust—ordinary smells, unimportant enough to feel safe.

No one vanished. No walls shook. That was victory enough for the first night.

Chapter 2

Small Mercies

Hope's Journal Day 2 – 3:45 a.m.
The Rusted Mirror

Couldn't sleep. Too much pain. Weeded through my fistful of paperwork. Miracles never cease.

In it, I found the spine X-rays in a folder stamped "Sato/2009."

I didn't remember the year until the insurance code whispered Rhode Island—the year I lost Jemma and Fowley, the year Dad's heart gave out, the year Amy and Paul slipped me groceries and a basement key I called providence.

I never named the pain.

The bishop said, "Three kids back-to-back—of course your body's tired." Jim echoed years later, "You're just soft now. Fragile."

Dr. Sato said, "Multiple untreated fractures," tracing a ghost-white line down my coccyx, pausing at a shadow along C4. "Whiplash," he murmured. "Or strangulations. Looks like multiple. No one time could do this damage."

Tears blurred the films; I pulled the bathrobe tighter, a lifeline of terrycloth against the flood of memories.

I whispered to myself, "Childbirth."

An imaginary Dr. Sato rocked his head side to side in my mind's eye—slow, almost tender— "Really, Hope? Lying to yourself, or to me, all these years?"

Tonight, the kitchen hums—fluorescent and unforgiving. My tailbone throbs if I sit too long; the ache in my neck isn't wear and tear—it's strangulation history carved between and in my bones.

They made me forget the violence. They normalized the inhumane. The mainstream Mormons baptized my skeleton wrapped in knowing silence.

I was there when it all happened.

How could I have forgotten what they shushed and sanctified? How was the fire once in me brain-blended and beaten out?

History was rewritten. Even my brain re-engineered to forget the horrific parts that make me – me.

No more.

I am remembering now.

***

First light seeped through warped shutters, stirring dust motes like tiny lanterns. Hope woke sticky on the floral sofa. Upstairs, children breathed in uneven chorus; the second floor had trapped the night's heat.

8:15 a.m. Gravel popped outside. Hope peered through the screen door, expecting Amy's sedan. Instead, a sun-bleached SUV eased up the lane. Out stepped a tall man with sandy hair and a steady carpenter's gait—laundry basket of stainless-steel pots balanced on his hip. The passenger door swung wide; a woman with a broad, white smile hopped down, cradling a plush robin-egg- blue robe.

Hope tightened the thin belt of her still-from-Maine-duffel-musty-Dinty-Motel-smoke-filled-bathrobe. "Can I help you?"

The woman offered the robe in her arms to Hope like an ordination stole. She sang in a Southern drawl, "Morning! I'm Nicole—most folks call me Nikki. This is my husband, Tom. Amy and Paul are my in-laws. They sent us ahead as reinforcements."

Hope blinked and stammered. "I didn't know Amy had any children in New Jersey. Tom, you must be one of Paul and Amy's sons? Wow!" A flicker of encouragement stirred deep—her Dad still guiding, perhaps.

"Surprise." Nikki's laugh was wind-chime soft. "Paul's texting directions for pipe-flushing. Tom here knows a P-trap from a bear trap, so we'll get clean water. Meanwhile, let's stock your kitchen," she chimed softly as she gingerly rested the thickly piled downy robe for Hope on the sofa's arm, somehow knowing where Hope had agonizingly attempted rest.

Tom hefted the basket past and behind Nikki. "Got mugs, forks, a skillet that only sticks on Sundays." Hope slid a skillet across the stove's warped burner ring, wincing as metal scraped enamel; old grease met peppermint dish soap in a scent that felt like someone had already prayed over breakfast.

Upstairs, boards creaked: Sebastian checking the perimeter; Emma coaxing twins from the heat-tangled sheets; Sammy thumping down steps, half asleep, muttering, "Is breakfast here?"

Hope smiled, tears dampening her cheeks—a mix of gratitude and fresh, confused faith. Outside, cicadas tuned up for another hot New Jersey day.

The screen door thumped twice behind Hope before she believed dawn was really unfolding in her favor. Nikki's SUV now idled beside the porch, its hatch yawning like a cornucopia: boxes of stainless-steel pots, mismatched plates, mason-jar cups, a sagging grocery sack of thick new bath towels (fresh peppermint scent already overtaking the must of the now permanently smoke-stained bag Hope packed in Maine and had relied on for months at the Dinty Motel and the Domestic Violence Hotel Voucher). Tom balanced a rust-flecked pipe wrench across his shoulder, army boots crunching gravel.

9:05 a.m. Pipe-flushing baptism

"Water main's probably iron," he said, kneeling at the outdoor spigot Sebastian had used the night before. Leo handed over a flashlight; Sebastian passed the hose coupler like a surgeon's scalpel. Matthew hovered with the intensity of a shuttle-launch tech.

Tom cranked the valve. Muddy sludge belched for ten seconds, then cleared to a faint amber before turning to glass. "Let it run till it stops foaming," he coached. "Mineral sediment, nothing worse—I tasted the hose water inside the line."

Hope exhaled; the sound felt like glass shattering in her chest. Anna peeked from the porch, towel cape billowing, and whispered, "No more tea bath?"

"Just water," Hope managed.

9:15 a.m. Journal Entry – Where Did the Blood Fall?

I was taught that Jesus atoned for my sins in Gethsemane. That He bled from every pore in the garden. That He died spiritually there — not on the cross. There's even a hymn about it. But that's not what the their Bible says. Scripture says He wept in the garden. He surrendered there. In anticipation of what He knew would come to pass, He sweat blood from every pore, in Godly knowledge of what He knew He was about to endure.

But the blood poured out on the cross, and the stripes He bore before the crucifixion was different. That's when the Temple curtain tore from top to bottom. No longer to keep His people out of God's presence, but to invite us into relationship. That's where the sky blackened when The Father had to turn away from every blemish His Son became that He abhorred. That's where The Savior said, "It is finished." Not in the grove of pressing olive branches — but under Roman spikes turned in by Jewish religious leaders for all who would claim Him as their Risen Messiah, Lord.

The Mormons or whatever they name themselves now, say that the cross was a symbol of death. But to me now, it's the place where death died. And yet even as I write this, I still hear the Latter-Day-Saint hymns in my head. I still picture Him kneeling in a garden — instead of hanging for me. I cannot grasp what is happening. There is something awakening in me that I do not understand.

9:25 a.m. Kitchen resurrection

Inside, the Lord orchestrated a quiet miracle. Hope slid the largest stainless-steel, freshly sudsed skillet across the stove's warped burner ring, testing each flame, as Nikki unpacked utensils: forks with meadow-lily handles, chipped-rim soup spoons, and knives that actually serrated. She lined mason jars by the sink like votive candles.

Emma fetched eggs from the van's cooler, and young Molly cracked them—half shells, half yolk—into the family's new mixing bowl. Sammy carried a loaf of bread in both hands as if delivering an organ for transplant. The scent of frying eggs and toasting bread banished the stale-cigarette smell that still clung inside the kids' duffel bags.

Emma threw the once plush blankets from Maine into the washing machine as her mother had taught her, thankful for no laundromat trips and waits, and draped her mother's new plush robe over the chair, rolling its sleeves like scrolls. The fabric's sky-blue nap felt absurdly luxurious against Hope's road- dry skin once she touched it after her shower that evening.

Tom poked his head in. "Pipes are clear. I'll haul a few buckets through every faucet to flush the lines." He nodded toward Molly. "Wanna be my apprentice, with your brothers?"

Matthew's twin sister raised an imaginary wrench in fine military salute and headed out the back door; the screen door banged shut behind her.

First breakfast

They ate in mismatched silence at the pine table: four on chairs, three on sofa cushions dragged up as boosters, Hope standing—too pained and restless to sit—sipping clear water that tasted faintly of penny but mostly of promise.

Sebastian announced inventory: "Nine forks, eight knives, seven spoons. Means we take turns if there's stew."

"Or make forks do double duty," Emma suggested, twirling toast into yolk.

Leo speared a fried egg, holding the bite mid-air. "You know what this tastes like?" He shrugged. "Breakfast."

The room breathed out a laugh—unrehearsed, round, immediate.

11:45 a.m. Hope's inner swell

Creator, You multiplied furniture and forks overnight. The thought surprised her; prayers formed on their own without any Priesthood Leader to correct her. She pictured Amy whispering trust and obey and silently amended: ...and rest.

But rest buckled when her gaze snagged on the peeling paint above the window—lead dust waiting to happen, no AC against the August scorch, surgery in six days. Gratitude and dread caught in her lungs before her mind drifted to the remaining boxes of paperwork that needed to be sorted and tagged. Hope counted the blessings her family did have: shelter and togetherness. Involuntarily, her skin tingled at these two miraculous gifts, banishing thoughts of lack or physical pain. More than she'd had with Jemma and Fowley... or was it? She couldn't remember.

"Maybe these boxes hold more morning blessings," Hope's mind settled as her gray eyes trailed across the room.

12:00 p.m. Gift Exchange & Planning

After stacking the dishes for handwashing in crisp apple scented dish soap from Tom and Nikki's box of household surprises, Nikki opened a manila envelope.

"Mom—Amy—sent the older kids something." She slid out seven sets of cream-colored cards ring-bound with twine. Each card read: Who I Am in Christ—forty identity statements penned in Amy's curly script, no source cited. "Fresh wording, a different truth from what Amy says you all are coming from," she explained softly. "I pray this truth gives you more peace," she whispered.

Emma's eyes widened; Leo flipped through the pages like trading cards.

Sebastian traced a line: **I am strong and courageous.** Molly mouthed, **"New creation."**

Nikki followed with a thin folder: "Thirty Hebrew names of God—each with a verse. The youth pastor uses them like flash cards." She handed the set to Leo. "The first name is **Yahweh-Nissi—God my Banner.** Fits the hose- shower victory, right?"

Hope watched understanding flicker across Leo's face—confusion yielding to interest. He passed the cards to Sebastian, who felt a shock of disbelief.

"Be right back," Nikki sang. "Mom and Dad sent down a big surprise for you, Hope. I think you'll love this. Hmm. Tallest man here—Leo, right? I need your help with this one," she hollered over her shoulder, the porch door closing fast behind her. Shortly, she re-emerged, Leo triumphantly hoisting a heavy wooden box that smelled of cedar, pine tar, and something vaguely familiar to Hope—a comfort and a question lingering in her nose.

Tom re-entered, wiping rust water from his arms. "Lines are flushing clean. Should stay clear if you run the faucets for a minute every morning."

"That box is from your Dad, Hope. His house, his box. Dad sent it down with Mom's things for you," Tom continued. **"Seems it's been waiting for you all these years.** He'd hidden it behind a stone near the bottom right of the hearth he built. No one knew it was there until this week when they were prepping his—er, your house—for the next tenants and realized some of the stonework was coming loose. They found this when they were re- mortaring."

Hope ached with excitement, grief, and other feelings she could not voice as she slid her hand around the puzzle clasp. She and her Dad loved doing puzzles when she was little.

Hope traced the brass hasp. Cedar oil glistened in the morning heat, releasing the smell of her father's workshop—sawdust, pipe smoke from his past, the memory of Sunday hymns played on a scratched record player.

Inside, the children circled the chest like cautious astronomers. Leo hovered near Hope while she unlatched the lid; the hinges sighed awake.

The top layer revealed a folded U.S. flag that once draped Gramps's casket, its stars still crisp. Beneath lay a velvet pouch holding marbled sea glass—the shards he called broken truths made beautiful.

Anna lifted an iridescent lavender fragment, its edges tumbled smooth. "Like tiny mirrors, but kinder," she murmured.

Further down lay four yellowed journals, their spines cracked, and nestled against them was a sealed envelope with Hope's name in

Gramps's angular hand. Hope's throat cinched. Not now. She slid the envelope beneath a journal, unseen by the children, a knot she would untie later.

Nikki re-entered, the screen door flapping shut behind her again.

"Fans," Nikki added to the mercy miracles that seemed endless to Hope. "We brought box fans for tonight. AC later if we find one that fits these windows."

Hope managed, "I don't know how to repay—"

"Family doesn't invoice," Tom said. "Besides, breakfast was on you." He patted his stomach.

12:45 p.m. Noon-Hour Sea-Glass Mail

Breakfast for lunch became a math lesson: Sebastian calculated pancake ratios; Molly practiced thirds by dividing banana slices. Hope wrote fractions on a paper plate with a Sharpie—sea-glass geometry—while online job boards loaded on Nikki's refurbished PC she'd donated to the family. Data- entry listings blurred as sitting needles shot down her hip. She stood, shifted her weight, and whispered to herself, "The true Savior knows my pain and more. Please be with me, Lord."

Matthew squinted. "If God doesn't lie, but they... the Mormons do... are they still on the Lord's team?"

Leo doodled in the margin of his history worksheet: a red-brick meeting house strangled by thick smoke. He shaded the dragon-cloud darker until the graphite broke.

Hope paused to steady her words before she spoke.

"You know, I'm not sure if they lie. That's a good question for Tom and Nikki. Why don't we ask when we go to church with them on Sunday?" A box fan whirred in the window while the twins cut sea-glass-colored construction paper for future art. Emma stopped short, interrupted from sorting Gramps' journals by date, tagging post-it verses he'd copied in the margins—Romans 8 drifting across what looked like crackled yellowed age stains.

"Mom, do we go to Outer Darkness and never see Jesus or Heavenly Father or each other again if we go with Nikki and Tom to church, and not back to the Mormon Ward like Dad says? Well, you know… like everyone says?" she ventured.

Hope slowed as she folded laundry, each towel smelling of Nikki's peppermint detergent. Pain flickered low but persistent; the nerve pills in her pocket rattled. She hesitated—if she swallowed one, the afternoon would vanish in a fog along with her response to Emma and her family. Pain is temporary; motherhood is permanent. The bottle stayed closed. She would give it to Nikki or Tom. She would let her pain draw her closer to her Savior.

"You know," Hope tried to sound casual as she continued, "Your Gramps did not grow up in an LDS or Mormon upbringing, and neither did I. But I've been thinking about the same things. I'm sorry. As your Mom, it hurts when I don't have the answers to tough questions like these, Em. Would you like to fast and pray with me to find out? God's the only one with that answer. Don't you think?"

"Hey, that's a great idea! Just like in the book of James when Prophet Joseph asked what Church to join, and Jesus said none, and then they found the gold brass plates!" Sebastian joined in, saluting the heavens and singing **Hail To The Man**, Jim's favorite hymn.

A ringtone sliced through the air—Hope's phone. Relieved from her children's questions swirling and pressing heavily upon her, she stepped onto the porch, cool boards under her bare feet.

Sato Spine Reminder: Pre-op labs tomorrow at 08:00 a.m.

Tomorrow. Surgery day minus six. She pressed the phone to her chest, feeling the faint churn of fear revving again.

Inside, Emma's laughter chased Sammy's around the table, following fish taco stick ingenuity for dinner a la Emma, Anna, with plating by Molly. Nikki's alto voice had taught the three sisters a new chorus earlier that day:

I lift up my banner in Your name, Yahweh Nissi...

Hope shut her eyes and let the melody rattle the old foundations of her LDS/Mormon mandated blind faith.

Hope's Journal – 9:41 p.m. (later that night) Where God Is (and Isn't) – Hope's Kolob

Day 2—miracles disguised as strangers who really aren't.

Pain held at bay through prayer and praise—pill bottle still sealed. Dad's spirit seems to be here still speaking. Not sure how to feel. His cedar breathes through the house; sealed letter waits like a ticking star. His flag mirrors the night sky: countless stars cast in a vast deep velvet pond, a dark night sky but far from empty here.

Clean water. Skillet sounds = music.

Kids chose Hebrew names: Banner / Strength / New Creation. Still no AC—heat climbs stairs like hungry dogs.

Fans blow hot, but it's better than no circulation. Water runs clear; children's names run clearer.

Surgery in six dawns.

The banner pole creaked tonight—maybe just settling wood, maybe a battle cry.

Psalm 138:8 "The Lord will perfect that which concerns me." Perfect ≠ flawless; perfect = finished faith in the Lord... but which one? And is there a difference?

They told us God lived on or near a planet called Kolob — the star closest to His throne. That He was once a man like us, who earned exaltation and created Earth as one of His many offspring worlds. The planet Kolob was more than a metaphor. It was a real place. A directional beacon in the galaxy that pointed us to our Heavenly Parents' home. But what kind of God builds His throne on a solitary rock? What kind of Creator confines Himself to a planet in a system He designed?

The Bible says He holds the universe in His hands. That He rides the clouds. That the heavens declare His glory. My Kolob isn't a star. It's a question. A longing. Is this one of the lies I swallowed whole that I now have to spit out?

The real God — the One I'm barely beginning to know or remember from my Dad— doesn't need a throne of dust. He meets me in this blackened but starry sky. Right here. Right now.

Hope closed her notebook. Outside, cicadas ratcheted the dark; inside, her father's sea-glass pieces on the table caught moon glints—broken truths and unanswered questions waiting for morning's light.

Chapter 3

Lab Work & Banner Lessons

Hope's Journal – 3:12 a.m.

Splinter Logic

Woke to Jemma's voicemail—no words, only the hiss of an idling engine. Corbin taught her that:

Make her mother write the worst-case screenplay in her own head.

He knew from experience how hard stalking was to prove and rarely ever prosecuted.

I played it six times. A deeper rumble under the idle—Fowley's homemade pipe bombs? Mandrake's investigator said Corbin bought the needed components by the sack with his friends last winter and called it a 'chemistry project for Christmas with his kids.'

Blessing bestowed, son perfected.

Corbin once swore on this transcript—

"I'll use my last breath, my next seventy years, to make sure those kids hate you."

The Lord led my fingers to the Docket.

It didn't take seventy. A year and a half, ninety-two back-to-back filings, and I was erased.

Jemma and Fowley kept the promises drafted for them in these beloved boxes of my legal trauma, which I will now call Evidence.

No. Fowley wasn't oblivious to his explosive ordnance training.

They're twenty-four and twenty-one now—old enough to rent a car and sign handgun waivers in three states.

Old enough to keep making bombs.

I still refer to them as 'the kids,' as if innocence were retroactive.

Self-blame has a mineral taste as the sun rises in tangerines and roses. If I'd severed my maternal umbilical cord sixteen years ago, perhaps they'd have healed instead of hardened. But I let the slow burn consume us all.

5:55 a.m. Gray light slices through the blinds. The kettle clicks off, and for half a heartbeat, I expect Dad—Jonesy—to shuffle in, slide a mug beside my laptop, and rough thumb smudge stray toner. Ghost muscle memory. Dad's been gone seventeen years; the coronary hit in courtroom 3B the moment Corbin mocked his affidavit. I never signed a single condolence card; grief remains sealed evidence. He's never met these grandchildren. A stray tear plops into my mug, rippling the peppermint tea.

My hands land on the docket in the third bankers' box of papers: fifteen motions filed in sixty days. Modify custody, vacate protective order, motion #7: "Plaintiff exhibits unreliable, paternal testimony—hearsay." Even in death, the court labels Dad unreliable.

Corbin promised he'd file until the paper stack buried us. I can still hear him, phone hot against my ear inside the shelter—

"You might have 'your kids' for a while, but I will file something every day, every week, every month, and twice on Saturdays until those kids are mine! Then you'll never see them again."

His cadence lives beneath my sternum like a second pulse. The judges and the court allowed him to keep that promise—through court-ordered call logs, third-party flying monkeys, and then supervised reunification visits with a female university cheerleader.

Seventeen years of my maternal umbilical cord became the noose around my youngest children—and my neck; sanctioned by judges who watched him twist it.

I should have severed every thread of my maternity for Jemma and Fowley the day Corbin won custody. If I had, would Jemma still dream of harming us? Would Fowley still flinch at nothing to stop him from extinguishing the lives of my miracle children? Self-blame tastes like copper, but anger won't cauterize this wound.

My old attorney friend Mandrake rings at nine. "Hope, artillery incoming," he says. "You could still run—Sweden processes asylum for those of Swedish descent." I taste metal again.

I print the name change and Social Security number change motions for the eight of us. Me and my children. Laser heat stings my fingertips. There's no calloused thumb to wipe the blood this time. Only me and the ghost of my father. I stifle a sob long buried.

Tonight, I will laminate Dad's ignored affidavit and staple it to motion #7. Let them call a dead man's pulse irrelevant; his words still weigh more than Corbin's breath.

Tomorrow, I file all of this—for Dad, for the kids, for the fractures that were never treated and didn't set right.

I remember. They won't forget you, Dad.

Dawn: I complete the DMV request, attach the cell phone tower dump subpoena, and pored through the SEC's now-public 13F disclosures and shell company records in the dark. Then I add the voicemail mp3—Exhibit C2. Paper and ink against pipe bombs. May the inked paper win.

If headlights sweep my window later tonight while the children sleep, I will not open the curtains. I will keep typing. Let the glow of this screen testify I stayed alive long enough to file myself.

The sun climbed, stalled, and hovered over the pine barrens like a pot lid pressing steam. By four-thirty this morning, the farmhouse's second floor had become a slow cooker; the donated box fan Tom found in his SUV stirred the warm air. Hope rolled towels, soaked them in the now-clear tap water, and draped one over each window frame. The evaporation offered a whisper of cool—just enough to keep her children's sweat from beading into despair.

Nikki arrived at 8 a.m. like a mix of Florence Nightingale and military mess chef, infused with the spirit of a former Carolina homecoming queen. Downstairs, she sizzled the skillet, intuitively making more than manna for bodies and spirits. The waft of melted butter frying thick slices of homemade bread for peanut butter and honey sandwiches held Hope captive long enough to break away from organizing papers, loads of laundry, and unpacking the family van; grateful for the crisp linen-scented detergent and woolen laundry drying balls from the Gideon's bag of supplies. The smell of sticky butter and cinnamon drifted up the stairwell, coaxing even Sebastian to abandon his screwdriver inventory and rejoin humanity.

Drowsy Afternoon

After sandwiches, the heat wrapped the house in velvet. Emma sprawled faced down on the queen mattress beside the twins, reading

Who I Am in Christ cards aloud like bedtime stories.

"I am strong and courageous."

Matthew added sound effects: "Raaawrr!"

"I am healed."

Leo, perched on a windowsill, whispered, "Working on it."

"I am a new creation."

Molly clapped once—her quiet thunder echoed in Hope's heart.

Sammy dozed mid-verse, thumb locked behind his ear. Even Leo's restlessness sagged; he drifted sideways, eyelids heavy. Hope tucked the plush robe under her own cheek on the downstairs sofa and closed her eyes. Humidity slicked her skin. This house didn't feel like an enemy but a haven for the first time in her life. The children felt it too. The farmhouse sighed: first real home.

Night 2 – Invisible Furnace

Heat snapped her awake at midnight, or so it felt. Boards creaked overhead; Hope surfaced from half-sleep, heart thudding. The box fan rattled on its middle setting, pushing tepid air in lazy circles. Through the open window, the outside night was cooler—barely—but mosquitoes pressed against the screen in search of dreamers' skin.

Hope padded upstairs. Emma slept diagonally, one arm around Molly. Matthew had cast off Leo's T-shirt, searching for cooler cotton. Leo lay half-awake, counting ceiling dots of streetlight glare.

"Can't sleep," he said.

"Think we're all glucose and adrenaline," Hope whispered, unaware of the weight of the darkened silhouette in Leo's nightmare dreams. She dampened a washcloth and pressed it to his forehead. Leo's eyelids fluttered shut; a small hum of relief slipped from both their parted lips.

She checked each child—pulse of fingers on forehead, breath on the back of the hand—then returned downstairs. The sofa springs felt hotter than the pavement outside Dinty Motel, but she wrapped her father's flannel over the plush robe and lay on them both as a makeshift mattress on the sagging sofa.

Pre-dawn Butterflies Day 4 – Hope's Journal

Ledger of Ashes

1:00 a.m. Can't sleep. Sold the Cooleridge Street brownstone in Cambridge ages ago to fund legal fees—$894 K gone in three retainer payments and co- payments to counselors. Corbin promised to leave me penniless; the deed transfer officially fulfilled that vow. After that, I was in the red.

Overachiever Ruby Victor had penned that motion: "Defendant incapable of employment; therefore, unfit as custodial parent." My spine MRI stapled to the front like a scarlet letter. Corbin's thrashings caused my loss of wage-earning capacity, and his attorney labeled his artwork as my moral failure—I taste bile.

Note to self: scan the physical therapy bills, code them Exhibit D1. Add sworn statement: 'Disability caused by domestic violence injuries.' That will make them read every vertebra. Dr. Angelino to write a Social Security letter for all of our name changes and our Social Security number changes for the H.A.L.E. Act for domestic abuse victims, along with the children's counselors and the Domestic Violence Safe House coordinator. These last seven children will far outlive me... along with Jemma and Fowley; I know of no other ways to protect them. Corbin clearly taught Fowley and Jemma his lethal hatred not just towards me, but he promised that and more back then, according to this 279-page transcript from Judge Countenance's courtroom to the Judge himself. My eyes scan further through this stack of paperwork and gasp aloud as I read the print:

"I will use my dying breath, my last breath to make sure those kids HATE—you!"

And then Corbin repeating those words again in my tape recording of his voice played before the whole Courtroom. I note the section in Sharpie.

Several pages later, I feel an icy chill as I read my own response back to the judge. My stomach churns, and my vision blurs with salty tears at my words,

"No...I...must finish...let me finish. It's as if Jemma and Fowley are not...it's as if they are not my own children. Do they hate me now? There are degrees of hate. Full-blown hatred, no not yet,"

and my words stop and start in a seemingly poorly glued mosaic, my blood the mortar and 'my children' the tiles as I describe Jemma and Fowley's first summer visit at Jim's house. I flinch as my body remembers them pummeling my swollen pregnant belly while Jemma watched Corbin use my womb as his punching bag when I was pregnant with her first brother, a third-trimester stillborn son, and again with Fowley.

I race to the downstairs toilet to catch the contents of my stomach; mostly water and acid followed. My body aches for sleep.

As my mind fades, I remember the first time I learned that the LDS Organization's Presidents, or Prophets, had routed over $30 billion in stock holdings through 13 shell LLCs, deliberately masking the scale of its portfolio — all while publicly claiming it didn't care about money— that they were men of modest means who were different from every other kind of clergy because they accepted no payment for their Prophecies.

"What kind of prophet does not prophesy but profiteers?" my mind wandered as it succumbed to slumber.

4:17 a.m. A single katydid chirped where no katydid had any right to chirp, and Hope jolted awake. Her phone's screen glowed from the side table:

Sato Spine Center: *Reminder—Pre-op labs TODAY, 08:00 AM, Providence, RI.*

Hope's stomach folded like damp laundry. In four hours, she would be back on an exam table, the antiseptic sting in her arm, signing forms she never imagined needing to sign again.

She scribbled a note for Emma: Hold down the fort; Nikki will pop by. Slipping into washed jeans, she noticed the kitchen smelled faintly of cedar and tiptoed upstairs. The children were still asleep, heat-stunned. Hope brushed Leo's hair away from his eyes; he didn't stir.

Outside, the eastern sky grayed into pewter. Hope slid behind the van's wheel, the windows already fogging. She whispered the only verse Emma had repeated last night: You are an anchor to my soul. The words felt ridiculous against her fluttering stomach, but she said them again until the engine caught.

Gravel crackled beneath the tires. The farmhouse shrank in her rearview mirror, the bridge glowing with a faint halo under the sunrise.

The Sato Spine Center crouched behind a hardware store on the outskirts of Providence, a low brick building the color of faded claret. Inside, fluorescent lights hummed like anxious bees. Hope pressed two fingerprints onto the check-in tablet. The receptionist glanced at the screen, noted the alias "Hope L." and smiled with practiced vacancy.

Blood draw, blood pressure, consent forms. The nurse's scrubs smelled of spearmint gum; the tourniquet carried the scent of latex and old fear.

As the phlebotomist expertly completed her work, Hope recited silently, Adonai—Yeshua Messiah—thank you for making new blood out of my tired blood. The nurse tied on gauze and said, "All set," and Hope looked up, relieved with a smile too broad, to mask the earth quaking within her. She hadn't allowed herself to remember until this week why her following three surgeries were so desperately needed.

When Hope stepped back outside ninety minutes later, a wave of suffocating humid heat hit her like a tide. She limped into the parking lot, its asphalt glittering like hot tar. Nikki's SUV glided to the curb, and the younger blonde driver leaned across the passenger seat, waving a stainless thermos. With a southern drawl similar to Amy's, Nikki offered in a welcoming tone, "Tom and a buddy are coming for your van. He thought you might need fluids checked and an oil change. These fluids are for you. Herbal blend of tea—chamomile, mint, no caffeine. Thought you could use something gentle."

Hope flinched. "No, thank you." The refusal slipped out sharper than intended.

Nikki's brow pinched. "Allergies?"

"History," Hope whispered, her fingers tightening on her discharge papers. "After the twins were born, I took decaf herbal weight-loss pills—no caffeine, all natural, the label said. Bishop called it stimulants. Yanked my temple recommend on the spot. Jim's mother remarried in the Portland Temple a month later, and I wasn't allowed past the lobby. Later on, the whole ward watched me skip the sacrament tray for a year after as part of my disciplinary council. Those decaf green tea diet pills may as well have been worse than an adultery confession. Corbin, -er my first husband, never had such consequences for worse actions." Hope's cheeks heated as if she could still feel the pews staring at her with scorn and her children with pity.

She glanced toward the back seat; the kids hadn't heard. Leo and Emma were busy comparing banner sketches. Still, the old hot shame and terror pressed like a hand on the back of her neck.

Nikki capped the thermos, her eyes softening. "I'm sorry. With us, tea is just leaves and water. No eternal damnation attached."

"I know—" Hope swallowed— "my head sort of understands. But the bigger part of me still hears *Outer Darkness* in every cup, according to the Word of Wisdom."

"Understood," Nikki replied. She slid the thermos into her own holder and offered Hope a bottle of plain ice water instead. "No ingredients except mercy here."

Hope accepted the sweating bottle. The plastic crackled in her grip, memories crackling with it, but the water tasted pure and cold—nothing like shame.

Nikki leaned toward Hope and asked softly, "Hope honey, did you ever read your Bible?"

Hope answered eagerly, "Oh yes! We study the Old and New Testaments that Joseph Smith translated as he restored the priesthood. We read those.

They are the corrected KJV, right alongside the Book of Mormon, Pearl of Great Price, and the Doctrine and Covenants. It's kind of like how the Israelites have some of the Old Testament, but not the New Testament. Joseph Smith says he did even more than Jesus Himself could do when he translated all of these works as a modern-day Prophet to form the Complete Covenants and also when he restored the Priesthood to the earth after the first twelve apostles died."

Nikki coughed, nearly choking on her tea. "Hope, honey, where did you learn all of this?"

Hope's gaze drifted past Nikki's shoulder to the red-brick clinic, and words tumbled out like marbles on linoleum.

"Corbin—or Jim, I still slip—made doctrine our dinner bell. Every night after the twins were born, he opened the *Teachings of Joseph Smith* manual and quizzed us between bites of macaroni. If I hesitated, he'd slap the table so hard forks jumped. Sundays between services were temple-prep reruns: he recited the Word of Wisdom, and I recited back. Even decaf breath mints became 'spirit poisons.' But I held many callings. Nothing was a secret after the Temple. My Priesthood Leaders and the Sister taught me everything that Corbin and Jim did. We were taught that after Jesus died and the apostles were gone, everything — like all of Christianity — fell apart," Hope said. "That the authority was lost. That every church since then was part of the great apostasy."

Nikki's brow furrowed. "You mean... everything?"

"Yes. That's why Joseph Smith said he had to restore it all. Not reform it. Restore it. Like everything had been erased until the 1830s."

Hope rubbed the scar along her C-section line, where her muffin top poofed out.

"When the bishop pulled my recommend, Jim called it proof I'd 'lost the Spirit.' He told the ward I was a cautionary tale. People shifted three seats away on the pew. Anna was still in my arms as an infant—she cried every time the sacrament tray skipped me." Her voice cracked. "That's how I learned tea equals Outer Darkness—there is no hell for us who dare question. Even serial killers have a higher place of exaltation than any of us who would dare to leave our Latter-Day-Sainthood behind. It's the New Covenant made only through Prophet and Martyr Joseph Smith."

Nikki thought to herself as Hope spoke, "Pavlov had nothing on this Mormon shame."

Hope glanced at Leo in the back seat. Yesterday's sofa-leap bravado looked wearied around the edges—shoulders hunched, eyes circled from restless sleep.

Nikki pointed to the back seat where Leo, Sebastian, and Emma sat surrounded by cardboard tubes and poster board. Sebastian lifted a poster: **Yahweh-Nissi** painted in crimson marker, a crude banner pole on one side.

"Teaching time," he explained. "Pastor Reuben says every banner needs a standard-bearer. We've been practicing before you got home."

Hope's throat thickened. Disagreements led to consequences. She thought before she spoke. "Nikki, you drove them all the way to Providence?"

"Reuben's idea," Nikki replied. "Field trip on worship as warfare. We'll picnic at Colt State Park after. Kids needed wind. Like I said, Tom's taking your van and driving it back after. He wants to make sure it's running smoothly."

Emma held a Who I Am card against the glass: **"I am free from condemnation."** Hope blinked at the card pressed to the window—I am free from condemnation.

The words floated there, bright and impossible, like a balloon someone had let drift into a locked room.

Free?

Her mind still echoed with the Bishop and Jim's verdict—lost the Spirit—and with people in pews scooting away like receding shorelines. In her world, condemnation was the floorboard above the foundation: always underfoot, creaking under the slightest weight. Condemnation kept you cautious, starving for approval you could never quite earn. It certainly didn't vanish because a laminated card said so.

Yet Emma's face behind the plastic glowed with something Hope hadn't seen since before the motel, before Maine—maybe ever. Joy, unweighted and un- serious, as if the words were not theory but oxygen. A breeze slipped through Nikki's open window, lifting Hope's sweat- dampened hair off her neck. She realized the breeze carried no smell of shame, only salt and budding honeysuckle from the bay.

Maybe, just maybe, condemnation didn't have the final say outside the world that the faith that Joseph Smith and her Priesthood Leadership had built.

Hope touched the bottle of mercy-water in her lap, felt its coldness seep into her palm, and let the foreign sentence linger in her thoughts:

"Free from condemnation."

The phrase didn't fit yet, but it no longer felt like someone else's language. It felt like a phrase she might learn to pronounce—after a few more breaths, a few more banners, if there was an unchanging God who didn't trade His approval for works and blind obedience but offered it as a place to begin.

Hope set the thermos in the cup holder, exhaled a breath she'd been storing for years, and slipped down into the passenger seat. The day still smeared with humidity, but the breeze off Narragansett Bay threaded through the open windows, smelling faintly of salt and cedar—like mercy on the move.

****

The van's sliding door groaned as Sebastian shoved a poster tube under his arm. Colt State Park stretched before them—bay water flashing pewter, gulls slicing the blue. June heat still pulsed, but the shoreline

breeze felt like an apology for every motel hallway they'd breathed. Tom spread a faded army blanket near a stand of junipers. Nikki unpacked sandwiches, apple slices, a jar of peanut butter, and plastic knives. The Gideons had mastered the art of showing up with just enough.

Sebastian and Anna unfurled the crimson **Yahweh-Nissi** banner. "Standard- bearer testing!" he announced. Matthew saluted; Molly giggled.

"Lift it high." Nikki tapped her phone, queuing a worship loop from ARC's youth band—drums steady as a heartbeat, electric guitar droning one suspended chord. "Pastor Reuben calls this 'warfare in four-four time.'"

Emma hummed harmony under her breath, then let the note swell into open air. Leo caught her eye and, astonishingly, joined in—off-key but intentionally fearless. Molly twirled beneath the banner; Matthew ducked and reappeared like a victorious groundhog.

Hope hovered at the blanket's edge, arms folded. Each guitar strum tugged at memories of solemn organ hymns echoing off temple walls. Music was reverent, not reckless—her Bishoprics and husbands had drilled that into her mind. Her heart thumped. She scanned the path, half expecting someone in a suit to appear and scold them back into silence.

Sammy tugged her robe hem. "Look, Mom!" He pointed to a horseshoe crab shell at the waterline. "Looks like a knight's helmet."

Hope managed a smile. "God's armor," she whispered, immediately regretting the phrase—was that allowed outside Family Home Evening manuals? Sammy accepted it as fact, tucking the shell under his arm like a shield.

Banner practice

Sebastian planted the banner pole in a dune pocket; the fabric snapped, blood-red against bay blue. He spoke like a junior drill sergeant: "A banner marks a victory already promised. Stand under it, and you're on the winning side."

Leo scoffed lightly. "What if the wind changes?"

"Banner stays," Sebastian replied, his voice unwavering.

Hope observed that exchange—the younger brother schooling the older—and felt a tremor of unfamiliar pride.

Lunch & small cracks

They ate cross-legged: bread smeared with peanut butter, apples crunching. Hope nibbled a crust, her stomach too tight for more. Emma counted gulls. Molly asked, "Is there tea in apples?" Matthew rolled his eyes— "It's fruit, dummy"—and Hope's pulse spiked at the word *dummy*, but Molly only laughed.

Nikki settled next to Hope, lowering her voice. "Does banner talk scare you?"

Hope shrugged, her gaze on her kids.

"Everything scares me. They laugh like it costs nothing. I'm just waiting for their Dad and the Bishop to step out from behind a tree and write their names on some heavenly discipline list."

Nikki frowned. "There's no bishop here, just wind and a God who isn't tallying hot drinks."

Hope said nothing. The bay breeze slipped across her cheeks, salty and kind.

Van hand-off

After lunch, Tom dusted crumbs from his cargo shorts. "Plan: I drop you all at the Bridge House, take your van to a friend's shop in Red Bank. Quick tune-up, change oil, flush radiator before summer really hits."

Hope stiffened. "You'd drive it alone?"

"Promise to fill the tank and return it by dusk," Tom said. "No strings attached."

She chewed her lip. The van was her last illusion of control—paint peeling, but mobile. Yet if it broke down in August heat, seven children would be stranded. She nodded once. "Okay—but I'm trusting you with everything we own."

Tom's smile was solemn. "Understood."

Evening return – farmhouse kitchen

They reached the Bridge House by mid-afternoon. Nikki carried fans—one box, one oscillating—and a dented stockpot. The children clattered inside, still sun-dazed.

Sebastian tested the stove. Blue flame, no sputter. "Works better with a pot on," he declared.

Molly brandished a new plastic fork. "Forks are freedom!" she sang, stabbing the air.

Hope arranged sandwiches for supper—same bread, now toasted in butter. The smell coated the kitchen like nostalgia she'd never had.

Tom rolled back in at dusk, wiping grease from his fingers. "Radiator flushed, belts tightened, oil changed." He handed Hope the keys.

She blinked hard. "I don't know how to thank you. Back home, everything has a price attached."

"No price tag here. Paid in full," Tom said. "Drive safe. We'll see you Sunday?"

Hope nodded, waiting in the hot driveway as Tom drove off, waving him goodbye.

Heat-wave night

By midnight, the oscillating fan pushed pockets of relief through upstairs corridors, but the air remained thick. Hope sat on the sofa, a new robe draped over her knees, jotting in her spiral notebook.

Kids sang with guitars. Molly asked about tea in apples. Outer Darkness felt far for one heartbeat.

Van in not-so-stranger's hands—came back better than it left. Maybe trust is a muscle.

Today, Banner. Tomorrow, more courage?

She capped the pen, lay back, and listened. Upstairs boards creaked—Leo's restless feet?—but no footsteps descended, no bishop in the hallway. Only the fan's slow breath and the distant rush of bay wind.

Hope's Journal – 11:21 p.m.

Day 2 – After the Tea and Banner Day

She offered me tea. Just tea. But I panicked. Not outwardly — I smiled, maybe even said "thank you," I don't remember. But inside, I was a new convert with Corbin again, sitting in a bishop's office, being told that a single sip would cost me my temple recommend. And without that, I'd lose the right to be sealed, the right to see my family again in eternity. That's what tea meant. Not refreshment. Disqualification. And even now — knowing what I know, trying to learn this new gospel — it's still there. The fear. The rules. Never being able to live up to the "Be-est Thou Holy for Thee, Yet Not For me," The invisible list of infractions I've absorbed so deeply I don't know where they end and I begin.

Peanut butter tasted like Sabbath.

Kids called rust "history" washing away.

Banner snapped in the wind; I felt something inside me answer. I'm still afraid of Outer Darkness, but maybe it's afraid of more. Afraid of trusting. In anyone. In anything.

Tomorrow: AC or no AC, I'll breathe gratefully anyway. Feels like new oxygen.

Chapter 4

Family-First Worship

Carbon Smudge

3:04 a.m.

I spread Corbin's filings across the floor, black-ink blots on pine. If a court saw the pattern—every motion filed the same hour of day, the same bullying adjectives—maybe they'd smell the combustion.

Mandrake texted: "Hearing set for the 18th. Prepare summary judgment brief." I typed through a spasm—my left hand numb by paragraph four. Disability spider-graphs across my screen: disintegrated discs, nerve impingement, complex regional pain, tailbone so deformed it looks like a hockey stick, traumatic brain injury from blunt force trauma.

Corbin called it laziness. Jim said I was an overly sensitive hypochondriac. The MRIs and X-rays tell the truth.

Tonight's task list: (1) draft summary, (2) attach power shut-off notice as Exhibit E-1—evidence of economic abuse, (3) drink water, pretend it's solvent. If the lights go out, I'll write by candlelight like a settler, carbon smudging every page in red ink until the pattern burns bright enough for the court and Social Security Higher Ups to see.

Children status: Jemma posted a story on her blog—sunset over a shooting range, captioned

'family tradition,'

after a long rant about how she's

"never had a Mother."

Sleepless days and nights, unreturned court-mandated phone calls, and them laughing about

"no consequences here about how I talk or don't talk to you!"

and the click of the dead phone by my own children.

Fowley tagged a reel building PVC pipe into confetti. The algorithm calls it fireworks; I know better.

They remember what serves them, forget what indicts them. My blood runs cold at the speed of their selective amnesia.

I run my thumb over the charcoal print and imagine soot on my skin. **Dad used to smear furnace ash on the ledgers if a column didn't add up; carbon made mistakes obvious. I need that now.** Tonight, I draft a victim impact chronology: each forgotten night at Jim's house; every shaken-not- stirred Corbin bruise wiped from Jemma and Fowley's memories. If the courts won't protect history, I will engrave it line by line with my own court- stamped documents.

I chronicle history, page by page, until it feels like the match that lit the dynamite that Jemma and Fowley aka, "his kids," have. The adult children I bore and loved, whom Corbin's groomed for 19 years. That's about two decades of education ahead of my youngest. I'm in the fight for our lives. My Jemma and Fowley are gone.

***

Hope woke to a chorus of gulls arguing overhead and the faint trill of Emma's phone alarm—8:02 a.m. Sunlight already crackled through the warped blinds, gilding dust motes like fireflies trapped in amber. The oscillating fan still murmured, pushing air that smelled of salt, wood, and last night's peanut-butter toast.

Upstairs, the queen mattress creaked as the twins untangled themselves; Sammy shuffled across pine boards in too-long pajama pants. Hope inhaled, bracing for the stale chemical scent of the Dindy Motel, but the farmhouse held only the aroma of Nikki's peppermint detergent and pine sap seeping through window sashes.

She'd promised Nikki they would attend ARC's 10 a.m. service—livestream projected in the church gym, plus a small in-person crowd. Her stomach pinched: another unfamiliar room, another chance to be measured and found wanting. She glanced at the kitchen sink; water ran clear, but yesterday's shame still pooled in memory.

Wardrobe scramble

"Dress code?" Emma asked, riffling through the duffel of freshly laundered clothes.

Hope hesitated. Temple whites and full-dress suits for men in the Temple. Sundays code is reverent: only dresses for women, with her boys sweltering in undershirts, ties and khakis. Memories burned and flashed through her mind—sterile, perfect—but Nikki had said "come as you are."

"Comfortable is fine," she muttered, fighting against herself.

Emma chose cuffed jeans and a sunflower-yellow tee. Leo pulled on a Sixers jersey. Matthew and Molly insisted on matching plaid shorts "like picnic napkins." Anna found her favorite flowered headband and adjusted it to pull back her shoulder-length blonde hair. Sebastian inspected everyone's shoes, then laced his own with double knots. Hope's robe still draped the sofa. She made the painful trip upstairs, took a five- minute shower, and swapped it for her one good blouse—navy linen—jeans, and white sandals; feeling both underdressed and overexposed.

When Hope returned, Anna stood in the hallway, thumb hooked in an overall strap, waiting for her mother. "Is church like our old Ward, or the Temple?" Her voice quivered.

"Neither," Hope said too quickly. "It's... singing and stories. No white bread and water for Sacrament, er Communion, and no recommend needed."

Anna relaxed slightly and whispered partly to herself, "If not, why are we going? Is this our way to Outer Darkness like Sister Roberts said in Primary?"

Hope bristled. She had been a Primary Secretary and served as the Music Director. She was all too familiar with the rules for attending other churches that claimed to be "Christian."

After decades of being told that this is the One True Church on Earth, having given of herself until she nearly bled out without any real relationships left, she wondered about The One True Church.

Jim's voice blended with Corbin's and her numerous lay Bishops from decades past, while the Sisters, who were barely even friends, rattled her mind and crushed her spirit as terror gripped her.

"You know your Eternal Consequences, Hope. As a mother who has already lost two children on earth and more children to death to other forever families, you best mind your Eternal Consequences now, if only for your remaining children's sake."

The Bishop's door slammed in her memory, and the Temple doors closed in her face as Jim's mother entered to get remarried and Sealed. She felt herself involuntarily shudder at her daughter's simple questions mingled with her own flash of panic. She slowed her breathing, grasped the armrest of the floral sofa, and gently lowered her throbbing hip onto the cushion before she responded.

"I don't know, Anna. But let's look for a scripture in the Bible from Gramps' box that he may have outlined in pink or orange."

Anna giggled. "Gramps used pink to highlight? Isn't that a girl color?" she asked.

Hope felt a moment of freedom and giggled back as she remembered her father's color code.

"Oh honey, no, not a girl color here! Pink starts with a 'P'—'P' for Promises. Cool, right?"

Anna smiled. "That is cool! Did Gramps have a color code for the Bible?" she asked, noticing the underlined green, orange, red, purple, and blue verses mixed in with some pink and yellow as she let the thin pages fan past her face.

"Well," Hope recalled, "yes, he did. Would you like me to teach you? It's been ages since he taught me, but I think I can remember his code. He used it to teach me other things, but we didn't really study the Bible together for a long time. I think he was only interested after—" Hope stopped short, a memory flooding back of the sudden disconnect with her dad after she'd married Corbin and joined the Mormons.

"Here," Hope turned to a verse she'd looked up earlier in her father's cedar-scented Concordance, thumbing through the Bible to find it.

1 Corinthians 4:1-6, 'The Nature of True Apostleship 4 This, then, is how you ought to regard us: as servants of Christ and as those entrusted with the mysteries God has revealed. 2 Now it is required that those who have been given a trust must prove faithful. 3 I care

very little if I am judged by you or by any human court; indeed, I do not even judge myself. 4 My conscience is clear, but that does not make me innocent. It is the Lord who judges me. 5 Therefore judge nothing before the appointed time; wait until the Lord comes. He will bring to light what is hidden in darkness and will expose the motives of the heart. At that time each will receive their praise from God. 6 Now, brothers and sisters, I have applied these things to myself and Apollos for your benefit, so that you may learn from us the meaning of the saying, 'Do not go beyond what is written.' Then you will not be puffed up in being a follower of one of us over against the other.'

"What does that mean to you, my girl?" Hope asked, facing her ten-year-old daughter head-on.

Anna hesitated and then blurted,

"Mom, I don't know! It's so confusing! The Bishop—Dad—they say that they're my Priesthood and that they are my judges on earth, like holy gatekeepers of who does and doesn't get into the Celestial Kingdom. But this," Anna waved her arm over the Bible's words, open to both of them as if for the first time, "says that only the Lord can judge me and that I can't even judge myself. When it says 'do not go beyond what is written,' is that talking about the Book of Mormon and Doctrine and Covenants too?"

Hope could not promise her daughter a concrete answer. "I feel confused, too, dear," she replied at last.

"Your Gramps was not one to speak many words, but when he did, his words were powerful and resonated with truth to all who knew him. He didn't say much about the Bible or Church when I was your age. But one thing I do remember him saying is that 'confusion is not a work of the Lord.' Can you help me look it up to see if that is scripture before we choose our path?"

Anna agreed. She opened Hope's phone and used a search engine while Hope's slower hands thumbed through the Concordance she was beginning to treasure.

"Found it!" Anna cried. "Here it is, Mom! Look," Anna read aloud, "It's in the King James Version too, the one our Bishop and dad say is the only right one;

1 Corinthians 14:33, 'For God is not the author of confusion, but of peace, as in all churches of the saints.'

It's right here on this Bible site, with a lot of other translations."

"Well, Anna," Hope felt relief, "I know the Bible says that the child will lead, and I believe you have just found the answer to our next right step. Ready to go?"

Anna hesitated. "Will they make fun of me for my weight here too?"

Her mother's heart ached with sympathy as she replied softly, "I won't promise what I can't keep. But we already have the Lord's answer to what happens if anyone does judge you, from the verse in Gramps' Bible passage just before that, don't we?"

Hope slid her daughter an Identity Card,

"I am chosen," as she whispered, "both by God and by me." She added, "Paul wrote most of the New Testament, and he says right there that he doesn't care if others judge him; he only cares what the Lord thinks of him."

As Hope slowly rose to make her way through the side door, keys in hand, Anna seemed to straighten a bit, her shoulders un-hunching for a moment as she stepped out into the muggy sun, her mother right behind her.

The ride

The van's engine purred smoother—Tom's tune-up tangible. Windows down, the morning air barreled through like eager conversation. Emma rode shotgun, a banner pole wedged between her knees; the crimson fabric rippled through the open window, drawing honks and puzzled grins from passing cars.

"Free advertising for God," Sebastian shouted through the wind tunnel.

Hope forced a laugh. Behind her smile, she tallied potential judgments: torn seat vinyl, her family's casual attire, her own unpainted nails. Outer Darkness, Outer Darkness... chanted an old corner of her brain, even as the breeze pried the chant loose.

ARC gym arrival

The church was a renovated cranberry-packing warehouse—red tin roof, wide double doors yawning onto a basketball court repurposed with folding chairs and a jumbo projector screen. An ARC volunteer in cargo shorts waved them toward a table of donuts and iced water. "Help yourselves—no strings."

Anna eyed a powdered doughnut, then Hope. Anxiety pinched her freckles. Hope nodded. Powdered sugar dusted her daughter's front like new snow; no lightning struck. Matthew took two, offering half to his twin, Molly. Hope waited for guilt's sting—it held off, confused by the sugar rush.

Nikki appeared from behind a soundboard, her long ponytail bouncing. "Morning, banner crew!"

Leo raised the pole; the crimson cloth fluttered. Nikki beckoned Emma and Sebastian to help tape poster boards along one wall. A youth band tuned guitars on the makeshift stage. The kick drum echoed off the rafters— heartbeat and earthquake in one.

Hope guided Sammy and the twins to the kids' corner, where Pastor Reuben knelt beside a rainbow parachute. "David danced before the Lord with all his might," he told them, tapping 2 Samuel on his tablet. "Today you get licenses to dance."

The twins' eyes widened—permission was a door flung wide. Reuben handed Hope a laminated card:

Hebrew Name #2 – El Roi (God who sees me) Genesis 16:13. Underneath was a question: Where do you feel unseen?

Hope's throat locked. *Everywhere, but here*, she thought.

Worship ignition

The band launched into a minor-key anthem. Emma and Sebastian unfurled the banner down front, arms trembling but determined. Leo stood behind them—standard-bearer stance, his idea of reverence. Congregants— some in suits, some in shorts—lifted their hands in a forest of surrender.

Hope hovered near a chair, her half-raised hand falling back to her side. Drums surged; bass thundered up her ribs. She scanned the exits—two, plus double doors. No organ, no portrait of Joseph Smith. There was a cross backlit on the projector, white on indigo.

Lyrics flashed: You see me when I hide in fear / El Roi, draw me near.

Hope's vision blurred; tears she hadn't anticipated pressed forward. She fumbled in her purse—no tissues. A gentle hand offered a napkin: Nikki.

"Okay?" Nikki mouthed.

Hope nodded, liar and beginner all at once.

Condemnation and admonishment buzzed between her ears.

"There are absolutely no brass instruments allowed during Sunday services, Hope. That is sacrilege. And the ONLY strings allowed to play before the Lord are the violin, harp, and cello. The only wind you will schedule to play for special performances is the flute. Now you CAN have any size flute, but my, WHAT were you thinking, Hope? A xylophone? Hand-bells? Ha! Next you'd have me sign off on a fiddler and timbrels, and then I would be on the other side of an ex-communication chair!"

The Bishop's voice was louder than the music, correcting her in her calling as music director while she arranged the first Christmas Services that long-ago year. Tears streamed down her face that she could not restrain. Fear and confusion equaled one hundred percent. Faith none. This round.

Racist verse collision

After worship, children rotated to breakouts. The twins returned from the parachute game carrying handouts: Psalm 139:13–14 — I am fearfully and wonderfully made. Matthew squinted at the verse, then at Molly.

"But 2 Nephi says God cursed bad guys with darkened skin. The curse of Cain. How can both be right?"

The question knifed through the humid air. Hope felt the room tilt. Pastor Reuben, overhearing, knelt.

"There's no curse in this verse, Matthew. A Psalm says every skin is wonderful. Want to compare?"

He opened a slim handout he'd tucked beneath his Bible. "Here's why it matters," he said, sliding the sheet to Sebastian. A headline read:

HOW COUNTERFEIT GOSPELS STEAL JESUS' IDENTITY

–written by a former BYU historian, © Truth in Love Ministries

Bullet points compared the biblical Christ — "the same yesterday, today, forever..." (Heb 13:8)— with the LDS Jesus, "a spirit -child who earned godhood." The theft of identity leaped off the paper. Sebastian 's eyes widened; Emma mouthed, "**political pyramid scheme.**"

Pastor Reuben opened the paperback KJV beneath the pamphlet and read 1 Samuel 13:14 aloud, describing David as the **"Man after God's own heart."** He reasoned, "Jesus' promised forebear is depicted here as having a ruddy complexion, unlike the olive and darkened skin that Jesus himself would have had; being both God and born Jewish, and living in the Middle East. Our Savior had darkened skin, as it says he blended in with the Egyptians during his time there after Pharaoh tried to kill him." Pastor Reuben flipped to Isaiah 53:2 and said, "According to everything I can read from the Bible our Savior looked common on the outside. Read what the Prophet Isaiah says here for yourselves."

The table huddled around as Matthew read,

"He had no beauty or majesty to attract us to him."– Isaiah 53:2

Molly's brow furrowed. "So... God likes every color?"

"Exactly." Pastor Reuben tapped the page. "Truth isn't afraid of questions."

Hope's chest constricted. Questions had always earned table-slaps and tribunal looks. She half-expected Reuben to bluster, but he simply waited, patient as the tide.

Leo whispered near Hope's elbow, "They don't freak out when you ask stuff." His tone held disbelief and budding respect.

Breathe, Hope

Service concluded with a quiet acoustic reprise. Congregants began stacking chairs. The children reunited, buzzing about parachutes and banner drills.

Hope stood under the high tin roof, feeling as though someone had opened a skylight. Light, unfiltered, nothing to dampen it.

Yet the old chant lurked:

"Outer Darkness…Mind your Eternal Consequences or I will mind them for you."

She remembered Jim's voice, mixed with other Bishops and Corbin's, and imagined Jim skulking outside the exit doors, wary of neon-bright guitars and doughnut sugar.

She exhaled—long, trembling, almost a laugh. Maybe Outer Darkness did fear light after all.

In that moment, she caught an unnerving thought:

If this cross really tells the story, then the Jesus Corbin preached and the "Eternal Father" and Scriptures Jim and Corbin quoted are counterfeits—board-room mascots for a corporate empire masquerading as a church. The realization sliced like glass; no wonder everything inside that red-brick ward had felt upside-down, joy-absent with the sensation of always needing to measure up but eternally falling short.

"They say that Gethsemane is where the atonement took place," Hope thought to herself. "I need to remember to look that up in scripture."

Fear and Confusion = zero. Faith won. This round

Picnic invitation

As folding chairs scraped across the gym floor, an ARC greeter in a sea-green polo clapped his hands. "Picnic on the south lawn—grilled burgers, slip-n-slide for the kiddos. Y'all come!"

Nikki's eyes lit. "Free lunch and faster friends. You in, Hope?"

Hope's smile felt brittle. Too many strangers. Too much sunshine. "Thank you, but we should get the van back. Kids need rest before the heat kicks up again."

Nikki read the tremor behind Hope's words and pivoted smoothly. "All right, y'all enjoy! We'll bring dessert by later." Then to Emma and Anna, "Save a dance with me next time!"

Van ride home – Anna's quiet storm

On the drive, powdered-sugar fingerprints dotted Anna's sunflower headband. She tugged it lower, cheeks pink.

Matthew, high on post-doughnut energy, drummed his knees on the back of Hope's seat.

"Pastor Reuben said we get to dance like King David every Sunday!" "David danced in linen," Sebastian corrected. "Technically undies." Leo cackled. "I am *not* dancing in boxers."

Molly giggled; Anna stared out the window, gnawing her lower lip. Hope caught her gaze in the rearview. "Sweetheart?"

Anna blurted,

"The kids at Primary used to moo behind me during ward parties." The confession hit the van's air like a stone in pond water. "They'll do it again if they see I took a doughnut."

"No, they won't," Emma said firmly. "Different church." "But same body," Anna muttered. Leo's grin vanished.

Hope gripped the steering wheel. "Anna, you are fearfully and wonderfully made."

Anna's eyes narrowed. "So why fearfully? Sounds like God's scared of me too."

Hope had no answer. The van hummed on.

Farmhouse debrief – Psalm 139 vs 2 Nephi

Back home, the midday heat pressed through window glass like a warning. The children clustered at the pine table Sebastian taped Isaiah 53:2, and Psalm 139 on one side of the banner pole, and 2 Nephi 5:21 on the other.

"Compare and contrast," he announced, activating his teacher voice. He also pinned Reuben's handout beside the scriptures.

Its title, **"COUNTERFEIT JESUS CHECKLIST,"** glared like a siren. Molly traced the checklist arrows— "extra books," "changing revelations," "pay-to-enter-temples."

"It's like someone swapped price tags," she whispered, "put the cheap label on the real Jesus and the expensive one on the fake."

Emma read Psalm 139, 1 Samuel 13:14, and Isaiah 53:2 aloud, emphasizing "wonderfully." Molly traced the word with a purple marker, then drew hearts around it.

Leo cleared his throat, reading the 2 Nephi verse about a skin of blackness. The words sucked warmth from the room. Matthew's shoulders tightened; Anna's fists balled in her lap.

"Does God change His mind?" Matthew asked.

Hope opened her mouth, closed it. For years she had wondered about the "curse of Cain" as mysterious justice. Now her daughter's doughnut fear sat like a smoldering earthquake in her chest.

Sebastian answered first: "Pastor Reuben said truth isn't afraid of questions. If two verses fight, one's wrong or misunderstood."

Anna's eyes flashed. "Then the Nephi one's wrong."

She shredded the verse copy into confetti and slapped it on the table like a verdict. Then she circled the verse on the pamphlet in red permanent ink:

"uncreated God, same yesterday, today, forever" (Heb 13:8)

"He doesn't change!" Anna's voice of truth rang through the kitchen, filled with new conviction and raw, jagged nerves.

Leo whistled softly. **"Guess the banner picked its side."**

Outside, thunder rumbled—heat storm brewing. Right on its heels came the growl of a patched Honda.

Tom jogged up the porch, wiping sweat with a shop rag. "Hope, quick pit stop—I want to swap your radiator hose before the temp needle climbs. Mind if I borrow the van for a few hours?"

Hope hesitated; then the confetti drifted from Anna's hand onto Psalm 139, a snowfall over wonder. She dug the keys from her pocket and laid them in Tom's outstretched palm.

"Bring it back alive," she said.

Tom tipped an imaginary hat. "Alive and cooler than before." He slipped out as thunder boomed closer, leaving the door wide long enough for a gust of wet air to scatter Nephi's confetti across the floor—proof, perhaps, that some words blow away easier than others.

Flash to ARC picnic – Nikki's debrief

On the church lawn, Nikki balanced a paper plate of watermelon wedges while relaying Hope's story to Pastor Marcus and three elders beneath a maple's shade.

"She can't drink herbal tea without panic," Nikki said. **"Temple shame runs bone-deep."**

Pastor Marcus adjusted his straw hat, concern furrowing his brow. Elder Chavez, a soft-spoken electrician, tapped YouTube on his phone.

"Heard of a channel called 'God Loves Mormons Too'? Might explain that shame spiral."

"Their videos are gracious, gospel-heavy," Marcus agreed. **He looked to the group. "Monday morning we 'll ring _ Ministries — equip ourselves before we blunder in."**

Elder Harper, a retired social worker, nodded.

"Love without knowledge can still bruise."

"Are we sure we want to pursue this line of exposure?" Pastor Reyes asked, pacing behind the pulpit. **"This isn't just about doctrine anymore. It's about race. It's about history. They taught that Black skin was the mark of Cain. That people of color were less valiant in the premortal existence."**

Pastor Marcus flipped open a laptop. "Washington schools boycotted BYU. Brazil built a temple they couldn't staff because of racial purity concerns. And that 'revelation'? It wasn't prophecy. It was desperation."

"But they're converting people of color by the thousands now," Reyes said. "Africa. South America. **They say those converts will become 'whiter and delightsomer' as they obey. It's still printed in their scriptures as doctrine; a current Cannon, nothing past about it."** Pastor

Marcus closed his Bible and leaned back. "Let 's table this. But not because it doesn' t matter. We need to let the facts speak. Right now we're here to decide how best to help a mother and her children in crisis."

Plans set, they bowed their heads for a 60 -second prayer, the breeze rustling paper plates —a small tactical meeting on a battlefield Hope didn' t yet know existed.

Evening storm & dessert drop-off

Thunder chased the humidity home around five. Hope stood on the porch, watching the sky bruise purple. First fat raindrops dotted the driveway when Nikki 's SUV rolled in, headlights haloed in the steam. She hopped out with a bakery box balanced on one palm.

"Peach cobbler—Amy's recipe," she called, sprinting up the steps. "Tom 's still tinkering with your van at the shop. He'll run it over tomorrow."

Hope blinked. "You already fixed it once."

Nikki grinned, damp hair curling at her temples. "Perfectionist mechanic. He's swapping a radiator hose so you won't overheat next month."

Inside, the children gathered at the pine table as Nikki unveiled the cobbler — a golden crumble that smelled like late -summer nostalgia. Anna hovered, eyes wide; Hope nodded permission. Powdered sugar from breakfast still speckled her daughter 's headband, but no one laughed. They savored warm spoonfuls as rain pounded the tin roof, and for a moment, dessert tasted like a pardon.

Elders' Plan for Hope's Transcription

While the kids scraped their plates, Nikki pulled Hope aside. "The elders met during the picnic," she said, her voice low enough for thunder to swallow "Elder Chavez has an extra monitor and keyboard. Elder Harper refurbishes PCs for fun. They'll drop off a setup tomorrow—give you a way to dictate your journal without hand strain and maybe stream a few things."

Hope's throat tightened. Gifts without strings still felt like traps, yet she managed to say, "Tell them thank you... cautiously."

"We'll keep it simple," Nikki promised. "No strings, just processing power and free software."

Upstairs—Quiet Storm Inside Leo

Night fell heavy and wet. The oscillating fan pushed damp air through the hallway, but heat clung to the ceilings like cobwebs.

Leo thrashed on his twin mattress, sheets twisted at his ankles. Half-dream, half-memory: the bishop's office, dark wood, echoing warnings—the Shadow Man—mind your priesthood, son.

He snapped awake, heart battering his ribs. The fan's shadow flickered across the wall like swinging censers.

Down the hall, Anna whimpered in sleep, unaware her own nightmares would bloom soon enough.

Hope, dozing on the sofa, heard Leo's quick footsteps. She met him halfway up the stairs, resting a palm on his shoulder until his breathing slowed. Hope asked, but Leo could not muster words. The rain hammered against the window panes They parted; boards creaked; no Shadow Man appeared on Leo's way back upstairs.

Hope's Journal – 11:43 p.m.

Day 2 Sealed, But Not Saved – The Priestess in the Mirror; Banner and Cobbler.

They said I was sealed for eternity. That I'd been made a priestess to my husband, a goddess in the making. But I never felt like a queen. I felt like a backup singer in someone else's eternity. The new name whispered in the temple wasn't mine to say. Only he could call it. And if he didn't? Then what? Would I remain suspended forever, waiting for a man who broke me to summon me to his kingdom? The Bible talks about salvation as a gift. Not a prize. Not a performance review. Not a celestial marriage with celestial laws. Just... grace. But I don't know if I believe it yet. I don't know if it's really for me. Or if I've already disqualified myself.

Tonight dessert arrived in a storm; it tasted like pardoned sins.

Different kinds of Elders plotting computers—still don't trust free gifts, but these fingers of mine ache less just thinking of a keyboard.

Leo waking from shadows—nightmares tangle us both.

Tomorrow they bring the machine; maybe I'll type **"free from condemnation"** and see if lightning strikes. Here is from today:

Psalm 139 (KJV) — David's Confession of Intrinsic Worth

Psalm 139:14

"I will praise thee; for I am fearfully and wonderfully made: marvelous are thy works; and that my soul knoweth right well."

(Some groups in ARC also read vv. 13–1G for fuller context, but verse 14 is the line Sebastian taped up.)

2 Nephi 5 — "Curse of Cain"–Style Passage in the Book of Mormon

2 Nephi 5:21 "And he had caused the cursing to come upon them, yea, even a sore cursing, because of their iniquity... wherefore, as they were white, and exceedingly fair and delightsome, that they might not be enticing unto my people the Lord God did cause a skin of blackness to come upon them."

(Most Latter-Day Saint printings footnote that phrase to link it with an earlier "curse" passage.)

Chapter 5

Bridge Builders

Wednesday evening, ARC church gym

The Wednesday potluck smelled like half a dozen counties: slow-cooker barbecue, cilantro rice, something Cajun with crawfish tails. Ceiling fans twirled above the repurposed gym, stirring August air into tolerable currents. Strings of Edison bulbs zigzagged from rafter to rafter, casting soft honey light over folding tables patched with vinyl gingham.

Hope paused just inside the door, children orbiting her like wary satellites. A banner reading:

MID-WEEK MINGLE

drooped slightly in the middle, as if bowing in welcome.

Amy Gideon spotted them first. Her vanilla rose perfume reached Hope an instant before the hug—ever Amy's calling card. Paul followed with lumber yard warmth, carrying a tote that clanked.

"Bridge pieces," he said, eyes twinkling. "One plank at a time."

Food Line & Character Beats

Nikki waved from the buffet, tonging fried chicken onto Styrofoam plates. "Y'all better hurry—these ARC casserole ladies mean business!" Her South Carolina lilt danced above the clatter.

The children joined the line. Matthew loaded macaroni pie until it leaned like Pisa. Molly chose watermelon slices arranged like fan blades. Sammy fixated on deviled eggs, whispering, "Angel eggs would taste better."

Tom leaned over to Leo.

"Funny thing—corporate filings list the LDS Church as 'The Corporation of the President.' You ever hear Jesus file that LLC?"

Leo snorted, ribs unclenching; the joke stuck, subversive and sharp.

Anna hesitated before the dessert table—a mountain of peach cobbler. She touched her flowered headband, then selected a modest spoonful. Hope watched, ready to intercept shame, but no one scolded; no Primary kids mooed. Anna took a bite, eyes widening at the rebellion of sweetness.

Leo piled ribs, cracking jokes with Tom about the Sixers' cursed season. Emma balanced salad and cornbread while scrolling her phone absent-mindedly.

Hope followed the Gideons toward the buffet line, her eyes snagging on a bulletin-board flier beside the door:

"SEC vs Ensign Peak: $5 million fine, $100 billion hidden—where's the charity?"

The dated headline hit like static. "If a church can hide nine-zero fortunes behind shell companies," she thought, "it's not shepherds we're dealing with—it's a venture capitalist dressed up to look like Sunday clothes."

Card Ceremony

Plates secured, they regrouped on the bleachers. Amy handed out name-choice sheets. "Pick one verse that sings to you. We'll laminate tomorrow."

Sebastian claimed **Yahweh-Tsuri (The Lord my Rock)** almost on sight. "Stability, engineering, makes sense."

Matthew and Molly wrestled playfully until Molly snatched **Yahweh-Rapha (Healer)** and Matthew settled for **Yahweh-Yireh (Provider)** with a theatrical shrug— "Somebody's gotta feed us."

Sammy pointed to a lion-illustrated card: **Yahweh-Sabaoth** (Lord of Hosts). "Looks strong. Lions ROAR!" he declared.

Anna studied the options longest, finally touching a lavender card: **El Roi (God who sees me).** She whispered, "Maybe He doesn't squint at size."

Hope folded her arms, marveling. No bishop's approval, no memorization drills—just children choosing words like treasures. Her mind flashed to every tithing-settlement interview: ten percent demanded by men who called it salvation dues.

"Mandatory giving for a trillion-dollar holding company," she realized, "while a woman who isn't even from The Church is handing out The Lord's identity cards for free."

Emma's Discovery

Halfway through peach cobbler, Emma's phone buzzed. She glanced, froze, then scrolled again. Her sunflower tee suddenly looked limp against her shoulders.

Hope's pulse quickened. "Em?"

Emma handed over the screen, thumb hovering as if she wished it could erase what she'd read:

Facebook–Jim Richardson "Life Update: Engaged to the extraordinary Marsi T., Bishop's Daughter! Wedding date coming soon—blessed beyond measure!"

Hope's stomach hollowed. The screen blurred; for a heartbeat, she thought the gym lights flickered, but it was her vision tunneling. Leo saw the post over Hope's shoulder. His face went stone. "Babysitter Marsi?"

Hope nodded mechanically. Tightness spread from her chest to her wrists. The children exchanged looks—fear, outrage, confusion battling for space on their cheeks.

Across the gym, Amy noted the shift and started toward them. Hope inhaled, aiming for calm, but the breath snagged.

Outside, a train horn wailed across the marsh—a long, mournful note that sounded too much like a warning.

Fallout & Night Watches

Shockwave in the Gym

Hope's fingers tightened around Emma's phone until plastic creaked. Marsi's bleached grin glared up from the screen, diamond ring catching light like a taunt. Jim's arm circled her thin waist the way it once circled Hope's, before wedding portraits and temple promises and thirty years of blind obedience to The Church.

Heat washed over Hope's cheeks; sound tunneled. The gym's buzz— laughter, clatter, guitar warm-ups—muted to a muffled pulse. Six children's eyes flicked between their mother and the glowing phone as if expecting something to explode.

Amy arrived first, tray of lemonade cups rattling. One glance at Hope's face and she set the tray on the bleacher step. "Walk with me," she murmured, slipping a steady arm under Hope's elbow.

Tom intercepted Leo, whose jaw clenched so hard the muscle jumped. "Need a job, son? Chairs don't stack themselves." Leo hesitated, then followed Tom toward a pile of metal legs—some task to pour anger into.

Nikki clapped once. "Dance-off in five minutes! Kids versus grown-ups. Matthew, Molly—show us David moves!" The twins squealed, grateful for the distraction. Sammy dragged Emma and Anna toward the parachute mural; Emma moved reluctantly, eyes still on her mother.

Hope let Amy guide her behind a partition strung with fairy lights. The plywood smelled of sawdust and lemon oil.

Hope's Near-Panic

Air refused to fill Hope's lungs; the room tilted. Amy pressed a cold lemonade cup into her hand. "Sip—slow."

Amy lowered her voice. "You know, Hope, Marsi's dad sits on one of the Church's investment boards. Marrying into him means Jim taps a pipeline— not a pulpit."

Hope felt the truth thud: custody papers could be greased with hedge-fund oil. She knew this truth too intimately; she had devastatingly lost everyone she loved to Corbin after the divorce papers were signed. The room around her seemed to spin, and her ears began to buzz.

Hope obeyed Amy, her lip quivering as she took a slow sip. "He's marrying her. My children's babysitter. They joked about her crush, and now—" She choked on her next breath. "He'll petition for custody again. He promised I'd never keep them."

"He hasn't won before," Amy said gently.

"Courts love fresh weddings," Hope spat, surprising herself with her bitterness. "Happy husband, stable home. I live in a peeling farmhouse with fans and pity furniture."

Amy gripped Hope's shoulders. "You live under a banner that says seen and loved. Custody rulings see more than furniture; they see patterns. And Jim's pattern is dismissive abandonment."

Hope's vision blurred anew, but this time tears cooled her panic instead of fueling it. She inhaled—wobbly, but sufficient.

Kids' wall of sound

On the other side of the partition, the youth band launched into an up-tempo riff. Nikki whooped; Matthew's sneaker squeaks echoed like playful artillery. Molly's laughter rang high and untamed. Their wall of sound built a buffer between Hope's dread and the world.

Leo, stacking chairs with Tom, cracked a joke about "chair Jenga." Tom replied with an exaggerated groan; Leo snorted, his tension easing. Hope noted the exchange—Leo gravitating toward Tom's calm.

Sebastian flashed a thumbs-up from atop the banner pole—standard-bearer and middle-child sentinel. Anna shyly spun her parachute corner when Sammy tugged it; for a moment, her headband's flowers fluttered like victory pennants.

Hope whispered, "They're okay."

"More than okay," Amy agreed. "You gave them the chance to breathe. This is true joy and love."

Hope mused, "For the first time in their lives, it seems."

Homeward drive

Rain-washed pavement glistened under streetlamps as the van trundled home. Emma sat shotgun, phone off, retwisting her sunflower tee hem. In the rear, Leo cracked jokes about Tom's chair Tetris score; the twins giggled despite their exhaustion. Anna leaned against Emma, her eyelids drooping.

Hope kept both hands at ten-and-two, aware of every breath.

At the farmhouse, Nikki's sedan was leaving. She had beaten them back, fans whirring in anticipation of their arrival; windows yawning wide. Inside, dessert leftovers cooled on the stove alongside a note:

Banners must fly higher in storms. Heads up. —N

Leo offered to bring in the banner pole; Hope nodded thanks, noting the slump of his shoulders once his comedic momentum stalled.

Late-night: Leo's restless orbit

Thunder rumbled in the distance but persisted. Leo paced the hallway outside Hope's makeshift downstairs bedroom—floral sofa still her perch. She heard his stalled breaths, the half-start of words.

"Storm keeping you up?" she asked as she raised her head from the box of papers beside her.

"Something like that." He hovered at the threshold, his silhouette defined by the hallway night-light. "Tom said engines need the right spark to fire or they stall."

"Sounds like Tom." Hope patted the sofa arm; he sat, arms draped over his knees.

"I feel like an engine that stalled tonight. Chair jokes only last so long." His voice scraped along confession. "When Emma showed the post, I wanted to smash Jim's face. But you froze, and I—I didn't want to make it worse."

Hope placed a tentative hand over his. "You didn't. Your brothers and sisters watched you choose humor over rage. That's more than any strength."

Leo shrugged. "Feels like a bad spark plug inside." He fumbled, not telling her about the dream he'd had again—the same dark voice and strangely familiar silhouette that was the true cause of his chilled sweat.

"Maybe Tom can show you how to change a real one," she said, half-joking. Leo's mouth tilted—almost a smile.

Silence settled—comfortable enough. Leo rose. "Night, Mom." He paused. "The banner's still up in the hallway, if you need to see it." He lay awake listening to the fan, anything but another nightmare.

Hope nodded, her throat thick. He disappeared upstairs. About an hour into her name and Social Security change paperwork, she limped upstairs and lightly touched the crimson fabric. Banner in storms.

Hope's Journal – 12:37 a.m.

Day 3—Jim is engaged. To our old babysitter. Storm outside, storm inside.

Amy's lemonade kept me upright. Kids danced condemnation into the floorboards.

Leo pacing—spark plugs of anger & humor. Anna laughed once with her mouth full of cobbler—miracle.

Banner pole creaks in the hall; thunder answers. If God sees me (El Roi), maybe He sees tomorrow too. Corporate prophets, corporate courts—but the Carpenter still builds honest bridges. Keep walking.

Hope closed the spiral-bound journal, listening to rain erode the night.

Hate Frequency

2:17 a.m. Fowley left another voicemail, this time static laced with a single word— "Erase." I loaded the file into software from Pastor Ruben and slowed it to 200%.

A metallic clink precedes the word; pipe threads grinding? Promises forged.

Hope recorded her own response into her trauma journal: "I still love you."

She deleted it. Love is gasoline to their fire. Mandrake says to ignore provocation, document everything.

So I log the call, capture a screenshot, and tag it Exhibit C-3. Inked paper against frequency.

Pain log: neck pain level 10; cervical burn level 15, tailbone off the charts. No funds for pain mitigation—insurance denied injection. It's painful to sit on a hockey stick.

Hope read further, musing to herself,

"I collapsed in court after Judge Bullock allowed Corbin's attorneys to cross- examine me for over an hour, and the Judge rendered his final blow. Let the record show Coercive Control, Abusive Litigation tactics, and no threats by Corbin, but promises made and promises kept. This is what led to my need for lifetime medication for Complex Post-Traumatic and current Stress Disorder. This is not mysterious paranoia or vague hysteria. Common responses merited by horrific circumstances."

Before dawn, I circle every adjective Corbin used—'unfit,' 'delusional,' 'morally bankrupt.'

I scribble counter-words in red: 'Court-battered,' 'blame-shifting,' 'lie,' 'survivor,' 'archivist,' 'fit mother,' and I write his own words with a cross-reference to the Protective Order:

"I would like to State...my Motto... Admit N o t h I n g! D e n y EVERYTHING! M A K E Counter-Accusations"

Red from another papercut bleeds through and stains the farmhouse floorboards.

At least the floor remembers. Now so will the papers for the Court and Social Security Filing.

What more proof could they need?

Chapter 6

Textual Showdown

Thursday pre-dawn to late morning

4:29 a.m. – Leo's Nightmare

The hallway night-light flickered like a dying votive as Leo jolted awake, sweat gluing his Sixers tee to his back. The dream was always the same, but last night added a new terror: Marsi at the end of an endless corridor, veil shimmering, hand in Jim's. As Leo ran, the carpet turned to tar.

He swung his legs over the mattress, breathing through the sludge of adrenaline. Rainwater drummed in the downspout, and the banner pole cast a crimson shadow against the staircase wall. He exhaled—one, two— Tom's breathing trick: in through the nose, out through hissed lips. It steadied him enough to pull on jeans. He tiptoed downstairs and sat with his mom, still categorizing and reading papers, before asking if he could have some instant coffee. Hope felt her heart shatter. Leo thought,

"Anything but sleep."

5:10 a.m. – Tom's Garage Rendezvous

Tom's friend's shop—a low cinder-block cube behind a gas station convenience store off Route 9—smelled of motor oil and burnt coffee. Sebastian, an early riser, volunteered as an 'unpaid apprentice.' Tom, brows lifted, handed him a spark-plug socket.

"Your van's firing fine now," Tom said, "but you'll learn on this '92 Corolla. She forgives rookie mistakes."

As dawn smeared pink across the garage windows, Tom discussed combustion ratios while Sebastian listened, knuckles steady on the ratchet. Between instructions, words slipped out.

"Seems like Leo is having dreams." *Click*. "I'm doing his chores. They multiply." *Twist*. "No fixes." His voice came out uneven, like an over-revving engine.

Tom didn't flinch. "Relationships recycle what really scares us. You steer them by naming the lie."

"What lie?" Sebastian asked.

"That you're trapped. Sparks belong to engines, not to fears or relationships."

Sebastian tightened the socket again. He changed the subject. "It feels weird we call the building a 'temple' if it's basically a corporate lobby."

Tom raised an eyebrow. "Heard that outfit owns more real estate than stuffed-mart."

Seb whistled. "Yeah. Guess the golden plates created a golden portfolio."

They worked together in unity. Sebastian huffed a laugh. "Pastor Tom now?"

"Just a mechanic who learned a few things about trauma and relationships after Desert Storm nightmares and adjusting back here; within my home." Tom patted the Corolla's hood. "And a bit about bad eggs from a friend's chicken farm."

Seb raised his brow in question.

Tom asked, "Ever wonder why or how 'Heavenly Father,' the Creator of the Universe, came to live on just one planet called Kolob? I dunno, Seb. I'm just wondering with you as we wrench. It says in my good book that He knows every star in the heavens by their own name, and me better than I know myself. It just seems odd that He'd prefer one planet over any other, much less be confined to only one." Tom wiped black grease from his hands and motioned to the sink where Nikki had laid out tangerine and walnut scrub.

"Here, Sebastian, this will get most anything off your hands," he said. The cool water and summer-scented bubbles eased Sebastian's unworked hands.

"Yeah, but I bet it can't erase blood money meant for Jesus," Sebastian half-whispered to himself, recalling the dimes he'd counted from his allowance.

"One little dime for every dollar He gives us, it 'tis not so much, no!" his dad had sing-songed during many family home evenings, igniting his guilt as his dad continued,

"We pay today so we live forever and are not burned up in flames like the chaff, but are as Heavenly Father's tried and willing wheat when his Son, our Brother, comes again!"

Deep down, Seb felt sick as the song echoed in his mind, drowning out the running tap water and orange blossom scent, swapped with the taste of coppery blood and coins he'd dutifully counted every time his dad paid him that twenty dollars a week.

Twenty dimes for twenty bucks. Suddenly, he felt like Judas Iscariot.

He turned back toward the farmhouse, deep in thought, his stomach heaving.

8:00 a.m. – Kitchen Debate Queue

Back at the farmhouse, Hope hovered over the stove, flipping peanut-butter pancakes—Molly's idea of culinary innovation. Pastor Reuben had agreed to stop by for a "scripture compare session" before lunch.

Sebastian spread library books across the pine table: KJV, Greek interlinear, Joseph Smith Translation, and photocopies of critical text analyses. He taped fresh pages to the banner pole: **Acts 17:26** (*one blood, all nations*) and a printout of 2 Nephi 5:21, Alma 3:6, Moses 7:22, and 2 Nephi 30:6, 2013.

Anna set up a lined notebook columned *Beautiful N True* vs *Ugly N Fake*, still clutching her El Roi card.

Matthew and Molly argued about whether peanut-butter pancakes counted as manna.

Emma, phone face-down, reread Psalm 139 like a mantra.

Leo lay sprawled fast asleep on the sofa where his mom had rested.

Emma scrolled an article on her phone and muttered, "SEC fined LDS investment arm five million dollars in what year—said they hid a hundred billion dollars in shell corporations."

Matthew's eyes went wide. "That's not tithing; that's pirate-hoard money."

Hope's spatula paused mid-air. "Jesus never set up offshore accounts," she thought, her pulse spiking.

She flipped a pancake too aggressively; batter splattered the stove. Inhaling through her nose—Tom's breathing advice relayed by Sebastian—she found calm enough to wipe the mess.

Reuben arrived with a satchel of colored pens and doughnut holes. Sammy cheered, declaring doughnut holes "tiny planets of forgiveness." Reuben grinned. "Forgiveness in powdered form—sure beats Outer Darkness."

Hope stiffened at the phrase; Reuben gentled his tone. "Ready to weigh scriptures?"

They formed a semicircle at the table. Reuben slid Acts 17:26 under Anna's "Beautiful" column and asked Matthew to read it aloud. The boy's voice trembled but held:

"And hath made of one blood all nations of men for to dwell on all the face of the earth..."

Sebastian laid the spark plug beside the verse. Reuben lifted an eyebrow; Sebastian shrugged, still caught in reverie. "Truth needs the right spark."

Reuben smiled, then set 2 Nephi 5:21 down. Molly traced the racist line with her red marker, drawing an exaggerated frown above it, and Matthew placed it in the "UGLY" column. Sebastian pulled out a highlighter and connected the two passages with a jagged lightning bolt labeled CONFLICT.

Reuben asked, "According to Psalm 139, what does God call His works?" Molly piped, "Wonderful!"

"And what does 2 Nephi suggest about skin color?" Anna's jaw squared. "That dark skin's a curse." "Can both voices be God's?" Reuben asked.

The children shook their heads. Hope swallowed—dry throat, pounding pulse. She expected more rebuttal pamphlets, endless footnotes. Reuben simply let the silence of scripture prove the point.

Sebastian tapped the conflict line. "If the Book of Mormon contradicts David, Isaiah, Acts, and Jesus talking in the Bible Himself, then they can't both be true." He turned to Hope, eyes bright, waiting for her judgment.

Hope opened her mouth, found no defense. She reached for her mug—empty—and set it down. "Maybe," she whispered, "some books sparkle wrong."

Reuben tapped the photocopied 3 Nephi margin, where footnotes cited "Church Educational System Manual," dated this year.

"Notice," he said, "even the LDS study notes route you back to their own manuals—a closed loop. Scripture that can't survive external audit looks more like corporate policy than gospel."

Anna exhaled, tension leaving her shoulders. Matthew scribbled Wrong spark under the Ugly column.

Sebastian's grip tightened on the spark plug—solid, simple, honest metal. It felt real.

Reuben nodded, eyes kind. "Truth stands taller when lies fall. And the banner still flies. You might want to look into analyzingmormonism.com"

3:12 p.m. – Emma's Phone Buzzes

The comparison session ended with doughnut-hole crumbs and colored lightning bolts littering the table. Pastor Reuben promised photocopies for their "truth archive" and headed for his truck as thunderheads muscled the horizon again. Sebastian began to open the website.

While Hope rinsed mugs, Emma's phone thrummed on vibrate. She flipped it over, expecting another meme from Nikki's youth group. Instead, a private Facebook message glared in bold:

Jim R.:

"Tell your mother the courts won't save her. Custody is shifting quicker than she thinks."

Three dots signaled he was still typing. Emma's breath lodged in her throat. She hit airplane mode, but the words had already detonated.

Hope turned at the clatter of a mug in the sink. "Em?"

Emma swallowed. "Wrong group chat." She forced a smile, but her knuckles whitened around the phone.

Hope didn't press—another crack to address later—but fear ricocheted inside her chest like trapped hornets. Courts won't save her. Jim had never needed courts to hurt her; his daggered words and indifference toward their children, favoring Jemma and Fowley, staunch returned Mormon missionaries and LDS Church members, mixed with his puffed and proud Priesthood power, had done plenty.

Suddenly, she recalled the LLC flier at the potluck— "Corporation of the President."

Courts loved paperwork; the Church printed paperwork like currency.

"We're not fighting doctrine," she stood frozen in shock as her mind spun toward truth.

"We're up against a five-star international government/corporate defense law firm with pews."

4:40 p.m. – Van Test-Drive

Tom pulled into the driveway wearing borrowed coveralls, grease smudging his temple. "New hose is in. Coolant topped off. Want to give her a spin before the storm?"

Hope eyed the sky, where slate clouds stacked like doubts. She nodded. "Kids, ten-minute break." Emma slipped her phone into her pocket, silent.

Hope climbed into the driver's seat while Tom settled into the passenger side. She turned the key, and the engine caught smoothly, purring instead of coughing. Sebastian drew his siblings near. Over 1,000 LDS scripture changes until their 2013 version. "Has anything else been erased?"

They trundled down the gravel lane, the scent of pine needles sneaking through the vents. Hope flexed her fingers on the wheel. "Feels stronger."

"Spark's firing right," Tom said. "Keep it topped with coolant, and she'll treat you well."

Half a mile down, Tom pointed to a pull-off facing the marsh grass swaying in the wind. Hope eased the van to a stop, the engine idling.

Tom cleared his throat. "Sebastian shared some frustrations about Leo shifting into neutral. Seems like he's trying to step up too soon, wanting to help where his older brother isn't able to."

Hope's shoulders tensed. "He talked?"

"He said the work corridors multiply with no exits. I experienced similar claustrophobia and anxiety after the Baghdad tunnels." Tom tapped the dashboard. "Mechanical fixes are easy; mind repairs need space."

Hope stared across the marsh, where storm clouds mirrored in tidal pools. "Trauma is cheaper than therapy. There's a year-long waitlist for trauma-informed therapy if you're on Medicaid or Medicare."

Tom tilted his head. "No way!" He exhaled, a sound blending amazement, gratitude, and disgust. He paused to think.

"Listen, at the VA, my benefits didn't come free; I earned them—two tours and more. I'm willing to share what I've learned—you're more than family."

Tom continued, "Here's what's even cheaper: talking before things explode. I told Sebastian he can work at the shop on Saturdays. It'll give him spark-plug practice and some safe noise for his head. Leo can join if he's ever ready. Besides, Nikki has a cousin in Nebraska."

Tom raised an eyebrow. "Heard that Latter Day Saint outfit owns more land in Nebraska than anyone else. I consider this pay – it- forward - time, to a fellow Veteran of a different sort."

Hope exhaled slowly. "Thank you."

Tom turned, his voice soft. "You drive those kids across bridges every day. Let someone patch the boards behind you. Besides, from what Paul tells me, you've seen more Tours with your ex than he ever did himself.

Skipping out just before war broke out to avoid combat with his unit. It's time you received some of the V.A. benefits he should have given you. What your ex did- Hope, being trained to kill that way, but using his Military training against you, those are War Crimes, by definition."

Hope glanced as his revelation struck her like ice.

"Veteran for Senate, Tom?"

Tom glanced away from her, his jaw locked, as he stared straight ahead.

"No, Ma'am. I just know right from wrong. And some Legislative Codes mixed in. What happened- what he did- wasn't just wrong or a crime- it was worse."

Lightning stitched the far clouds; thunder rolled a moment later. Hope eased the van back onto the road, feeling the steering tighten into certainty. She breathed in deeply. Tom's truths didn't sting – they sung.

9:18 p.m. – First Droplets & Emma's Confession

Rain began as a hiss, rising to a thousand-finger drum on the roof. Hope sorted laundry downstairs when Emma descended, her sunflower tee limp.

"Mom, I lied—earlier," she whispered, revealing the frozen DM. Hope's pulse quickened. She kept her voice steady. "Did you reply?"

"No. I blocked him." Emma's chin quivered. "Is he right? Can courts take us?"

Hope folded a towel that trembled in her grip. "Courts look for patterns, remember? It's up to you to outline your dad's pattern and relationship with you. You, Leo, and Sebastian are old enough to have a voice. Courts will consider your statements, but you need to write them, not me. I can't and won't influence you." She prayed her words sounded truer than Joseph Smith's gold brass plates felt after Seb told her about the ever changing LDS Mormon Doctrines her children had discovered with Pastor Ruben.

Emma nodded, tears leaking, anchoring them both in the present. Hope hugged her eldest; firm and steady. Over Emma's shoulder, she glimpsed Psalm 139 taped to the fridge. Marvelous works —truth mocked Jim's DM.

Hope kissed Emma's temple. "Sleep. Write in your journal with everyone upstairs later. We'll deal with storms if they come."

***

11:04 p.m. – Leo's Confession

Thunder had dragged on for hours when Leo appeared at the open back door of the kitchen, soaked from sprinting across the drive and lightning-lit yard. Tom, wiping down van tools on the porch, ushered him under shelter.

Leo's chest heaved. "Felt the storm... needed spark-plug zen." Tom handed him a shop towel. "Shoot."

Leo leaned against the porch post, rain veiling the yard. "Dream again—there's this shadowy man I know but don't recognize. Plus there's Marsi this time." He spat the name like oil. "Yesterday—when Mom froze—I wanted to smash something. I'm scared I'll become him- er Dad, or worse."

Tom considered. Wind rattled the banner pole through the hall window. "Sometimes nightmares reveal fears," He dug into his pocket and produced a new spark plug. "Spark plug helps your mind fire. Gap 's perfect, electrode clean. Nothing false ignites it. But spark plugs need grounding."

Leo turned the metal between his fingers. "Grounding?"

"Friends, scripture, breathing—maybe a goofy uncle who makes you sand rust off brake drums."

Lightning flashed; thunder crouched overhead. Leo managed a shaky grin. "Uncle Tom, huh?"

Tom shrugged. "Tom will do." "Thanks for fixing Mom's van."

"It just needed the right spark," Tom replied.

They stood listening to the rain until it softened. Inside, Hope watched from the hallway, unseen, palm pressed to Psalm 139—an anchor in a new storm.

Hope's Journal – 12:06 a.m.

Day 4—Before the Beginning. Did I experience War Crimes? Corbin's marriage? Before? Corbin never saw combat; did I?

Before the Beginning: **We were told we existed before we were born —** that we were spirit children of Heavenly Father. **That Jesus was our eldest brother. That Lucifer was our brother too.** That there was a grand council in heaven and two plans — one that gave us agency, and one that didn't. And we chose Jesus' plan. I've never heard it outside the Church. Not once. But I believed it. I still believe it. Or maybe I just haven't let it go yet. It made the world feel ordered — like I had a place in it, before I was even me. But the Jesus they say is in this church — the one I'm trying to trust — He didn't start in a council. He didn't get elected by siblings. He was. He is. Alpha. Omega. Not firstborn. First cause. **I don't know what to do with that yet.**

Tom's War Crime Legislative Code re. my marriage time with Corbin. Do Corbin's actions upon our children, Jemma and Fowley count as War Crimes, too? What about what happened to me; while Corbin was — in?

Fact checked Mormon Nebraska land holdings. Hmmm. Found that **Farmland Reserve Inc.** is the **top land purchaser** in the state over the last decade, with ~370,000 acres. Add that to the ranches — like **Deseret Ranch in Florida, the largest private landholding in the state of Florida—** plus **Mormon stock holdings in tech fortunes**… makes me wonder what the Latter-Day-Saint/ Mormon Presidents don't have influence over? Is there anything separate? I thought Church and State were Constitutionally not co-mingled. Has that now changed? How? Why is that legal? **For any entity that claims religious tax-exempt status, how can this be?**

Jim's new marriage DM to Emma rattled us but she blocked it.

Courts may see patterns; does this different God see sparks of my Spirit?

Leo was soaking wet; spark plug in hand.

Tom = steady grounding. Rain scrubs the roof; banner pole sings in the wind.

I need rest but feel restless.

Chapter 7

Wednesday Youth Wave

Phantom Salary

Hope's Journal – 4:30 a.m.

The Employment Specialist letter arrived yesterday— "capacity for sedentary employment exists."

If only sitting didn't feel like rebar driven through my spine and out through my tush. If only typing weren't like seeing the white and black fuzz on an out- of-frequency old television, with stabbing pain behind my eyes due to my frozen neck and arms that letter might make sense.

I flashed back to the cubicle job I lost 21 years ago: Corbin served a subpoena at the reception desk. I was fired for 'legal disruptions.' I had never been fired from a job before.

College delayed again after marrying Jim to be 'un-Sealed' from Corbin, even though we were legally divorced.

Mr. Magical keeps winning retroactively.

I tally lost wages while married to Jim: $875,000 in potential earnings, zero accrued retirement. Add that to Exhibit F-1.

Mandrake warns judges tune out numbers after six figures, so I write my other financial losses in groceries:

2,09G weeks of milk, 31,000 school lunches.

I attach the last trip we made to the Food Bank along with the affidavit from Jim, who took all his children and extended family out to a steakhouse.

Maybe they'll taste the shortfall for our children.

Task: draft a motion to compel the vocational expert to testify. Pain spikes; sensation in my fingers fades.

Dictate instead—my voice shakes. The software mishears 'strangulation' as 'strange relation.' Maybe it's right.

Corbin's kids check in on the blanked-out online forum: Jemma posted a meme:

"Your trauma isn't an excuse." 1,200 likes.

Healing or mockery?

I can't tell anymore with her. I screen-capture anyway—Exhibit C-4. Next I will try to rest. What will Marsi throw into the mix?

ARC Church Campus, Day 5, 6:42 p.m.
Arrival Buzz

The ARC campus bustled like a carnival: food-truck aromas, strings of patio lights, and a low thump of bass leaking from the youth wing. A "MID-WEEK WAVE" banner whipped in the bay breeze—surfboard font, teal and coral.

Hope's van eased into a gravel spot. Tom followed in his patched Honda, radio spilling classic rock. The children spilled out like pent-up marbles. Pastor Reuben flagged them toward the lawn, clipboard in hand, neon wristbands dangling.

"Scavenger night!" he called above the music. "Find clues, collect Hebrew-name tokens, win bragging rights."

Sebastian eyed a glossy flyer taped to a food-truck window:

"Church Investment Fund Tops $100 Billion—Wall Street Journal."

He muttered, "Youth group budgets run on bake sales; those guys bank like Fortune 100."

Leo snorted.

"Ticker Symbol L.D.$."

The joke popped like bubble gum, but Hope felt the subtext: gospel or conglomerate?

Molly tugged Sebastian's sleeve. "What do we win?"

Reuben winked. "Snow-cone vouchers—and honor eternal."

Matthew saluted; Anna adjusted her flowered headband, eyes darting across clusters of unfamiliar kids.

Team Formation

Youth volunteers handed out color-coded bandanas. Emma, Leo, and Sebastian ended up on **Team Sapphire** with Tom as the adult lead. The twins joined **Team Lime** with Nikki. Sammy glued himself to Nikki's calf, delighted.

Anna hesitated. Hope knelt. "You okay, ladybug?" Anna whispered, "My legs jiggle when I run."

"Legs are engines," Hope answered, recalling Tom's metaphor. "Engines move banners." She pointed to Reuben's clipboard. Anna squared her shoulders and accepted a **Team Amber** bandana.

Nikki knelt to tie Sammy's bandana. "Good news—no entrance fees." Hope caught the tease. "Unlike temple recommends that cost ten percent?"

Nikki's grin turned wry. "We tithe hearts, not salaries. Makes accountants nervous."

Hope exhaled, letting the bay wind carry her own nerves.

Clue Hunt

A whistle blew. Teams scattered. The first clue— "Find Yahweh-Rapha where He Heals"—and led the Sapphire squad to a first-aid tent. Leo cracked the medical box, retrieving a green token stamped HEALER. He fist-bumped Sebastian, confidence blooming.

Anna's Team Amber raced across a sand-volleyball court to unearth the Yahweh-Yireh (Provider) token hidden beneath picnic-table bread loaves. Her laughter rose when she beat two skinny boys to the clue.

From the sidelines, Hope watched as grins replaced grimaces. She clutched her El Roi card, pondering a God who sees from fields and volleyball pits alike.

Snow-Cone Aftermath

Team Sapphire won by two tokens; Leo spun a foam finger like a helicopter. Snow-cones dyed tongues neon. Twin brains froze as Nikki led them in the cross-eyed "brain-freeze shake-off" dance, each child flapping their arms like startled gulls. The crowd laughed—innocent, unweaponized laughter.

Tom waved a blue-raspberry cone. "Best part? Free." Sebastian asked, "How does ARC afford all this?"

Pastor Reuben passed by and quipped, "We trade on grace, not hedge funds." A few volunteers laughed, the line landing harder on Hope than they knew.

Anna stood beside Hope, cherry syrup dribbling down her wrist. "I don't jiggle much when I sprint," she admitted.

"Engines don't apologize for torque," Hope replied, surprising herself. Anna grinned and wiped the syrup on her bandana.

Pastor Huddle

While kids compared tongue colors, Pastor Marcus pulled Hope aside beneath a string of Edison bulbs. "Elders secured that refurbished PC; we'll drop it by tomorrow. Also—Love in All Ministries is shipping us study guides."

He lowered his voice. "Their newest packet walks through 'Corporation Sole' filings—shows how LDS prophets sign tax returns as CEOs."

Hope's breath caught. "CEO, not shepherd." Another puzzle piece clicked into place.

She managed gratitude, wary but willing.

"Tom says Sebastian's pretty handy," Marcus added. "I'm thinking of letting him help design the youth banner rack."

Hope followed Marcus's gaze: Sebastian demonstrating spark-plug gaps with a snow-cone spoon. "Handy," she echoed, her heart swelling and aching all at once for Leo, who seemed lost, and Sebastian, who had too much.

Marcus's voice softened. "The banner's holding, Hope." She nodded, eyes misty. "Storms keep testing it."

"Storms prove stakes," he replied.

***

10:47 p.m. – House Settling

The farmhouse exhaled a day's worth of humidity through cracked windows. Oscillating fans whirred like tired cicadas, stirring air that smelled of snow- cone syrup and damp sneaker soles. Upstairs, the queen mattress sagged under the weight of four exhausted bodies—twins starfished, Sammy sprawled like a starfish's shadow, Emma reading Psalms by phone light until her eyelids succumbed.

Leo and Sebastian claimed their twin beds; Sebastian's new spark plug gleamed on the nightstand under the sliver of light from the door.

Hope closed the hallway door softly and padded downstairs. She jotted a quick note in her journal—Engines don't apologize for torque—scrawling it in the margin and smiling at the odd poetry.

Browser history from earlier flickered in Hope's mind:

"SEC vs Ensign Peak,"

shell LLCs named after Nephite cities.

Forty years of "lay clergy" looked less like sacrifice and more like salary laundering.

"Corporate prophets build portfolios; Carpenter prophets built people," she scrawled in the margin and clicked off the lamp.

Rain made way for cricket songs; this once, the safe house sounded like ordinary summer rather than a haunted past.

1:18 a.m. – Anna's Nightmare

In the darkness above, Anna's dream began benign: a picnic table piled with peach cobbler. She reached for a slice, but hands yanked the plate away. Laughter swelled—the Primary kids from the Maine ward—mooing in cruel cadence. The picnic table morphed into a scale; numbers spun like slot- machine reels before freezing at CURSE. A bishop's voice boomed: No sacrament for gluttons. She tried to speak, her throat clogged with powdered sugar that tasted like chalk.

She woke mid-scream, heart racing. The silhouettes of her sleeping siblings blurred. Heat wrapped around her like plastic. Tears burned unfamiliar paths down her cheeks.

Anna tiptoed out, the floorboards sighing under each step, and descended the stairs where the house slept more deeply. She hesitated at the sofa's edge.

Hope sensed movement before her daughter's whisper: "Mom?"

She bolted upright. The lamp clicked on, casting gentle gold. Anna stood trembling, her headband askew.

Midnight Disclosure

Hope drew her close. "Bad dream?"

Anna nodded, swallowing sobs. "They—everyone—mooed again. And... the Bishop said curse. Like Nephi." She inhaled and hiccupped. "Psalm said wonderful, but the Bishop said curse."

Hope's stomach dropped, recalling the shredded confetti. She guided Anna onto the sofa and tucked the plush robe around her shoulders despite the heat.

Rain hissed outside, but the house felt hushed—holy, almost. Anna's voice shook, tears sliding down her freckled cheeks. "Psalm says ' wonderfully,' but Nephi says 'blackness' and Bishop says 'fat.' Which one wins, Mom?"

Hope brushed damp hair from Anna's forehead, her heart aching. "Do you know," she began, "I have a picture of me at ten years old—same round cheeks, same nervous eyes. I hated that picture for years because kids at school called me Hippo Hope."

Anna blinked. "They were mean to you too?"

"Mean enough that I skipped my birthday cake that year. I thought smaller would mean safer." Hope's fingers traced the faint scar beneath her C-section line through the robe. "But this body—soft places, scars and all—carried you, carried Matthew, Molly, Sammy, and before them, Em and Leo. It's a map of miracles."

Anna frowned, absorbing the idea.

Hope continued, her voice steadier. "When my husband Corbin married someone younger and slimmer, I thought my curves proved I'd failed. But curves were proof I'd loved—proof I'd lived. Your shape shows you're alive and growing, not cursed. Psalms says God stitches us together like masterpieces."

Anna touched her own belly through her pajamas. "Masterpieces jiggle?"

"Michelangelo's paint cracked with time," Hope smiled. "Art ages, art jiggles, art stands."

Anna's shoulders lowered. "Bishop lied, then."

"Bishop was wrong," Hope admitted, the words scraping her throat yet tasting like freedom. She lifted the lavender El Roi card. "God who sees us—sees all of us. He isn't squinting in disgust; He's counting freckles like stars."

Anna's lips twitched toward a smile. "That's a lot of stars."

"A galaxy's worth." Hope opened the *Who I Am* deck to a line she'd avoided until now: **I am accepted and Beloved.** She offered the card. "No mooing, no ranking, just accepted. Loved by the Creator of you, and the entire Universe."

Anna traced the letters and then nestled under Hope's arm. "Mom, do you think maybe God's banner fits around... wider art?"

Hope kissed her hair. "His banner stretches wider than any waistline or planet."

They sat together until Anna's breathing slowed to the gentle rhythm of rain, Psalm 139 echoed in Hope's mind—wonderfully made, no asterisk attached.

Anna traced the letters, mouthing each word. "Beloved sounds better than glutton."

Hope's eyes stung. "You are beloved. Wonderfully beloved."

They sat, listening to crickets filter through screens, until Anna's breathing slowed again.

"Can I sleep here?" she asked.

Hope nodded. She unfolded the scratchy wool blanket; it smelled of rain now, not mildew. Anna curled up, clutching the El Roi and *I am accepted in the Beloved* cards like night-lights.

Hope's phone buzzed—a voicemail from the state counseling hotline returning her 211 and Medicaid calls:

"Next trauma-informed pediatric slot estimated twelve months. Consider faith-based ecclesiastical solutions in the interim."

She deleted it, heart pounding.

"The very system that calls my sons 'triggers' unfit for a bed in a domestic violence shelter just because they are over twelve years old, and now my daughter a curse because of her BMI, would rather outsource them because we don't hold Leadership in the hedge fund church facade that seems to own top stock in the medical insurance companies."

The pain in her spine was palpable as always, but nothing compared to the knives now firmly rooted in her back by the LDS organization. The same entity that nearly killed her; while married to Corbin. The LDS / Mormons helped shaped Jemma and Fowley far worse than their dad, Corbin; ...oh, what about Jim's engagement? ...Our babysitter, really? Hope scooped in a billow of air and slowly exhaled to calm her racing thoughts.

Rain hammered harder; Hope tucked the blanket tighter.

She smoothed her daughter's hair, whispering Psalm 139 under her breath until the words became prayer.

2:03 a.m. – Phone Buzz

The phone on the side table vibrated—flat, insistent. Hope's pulse jumped. The screen lit up with an unfamiliar toll-free number: **877-CUSTODY-NOW** with a subtext preview:

"Specializing in rapid reunification. Attorney Richardson will—"

Hope's thumb hovered over decline. Richardson—Jim's cousin—had once boasted of passing the bar. A tempest of dread threatened to erase the Psalm victory. She hit Block. The phone offered no relief; the darkness felt suddenly thicker.

Upstairs, the house remained quiet—no more nightmares, only crickets and banner fabric rustling in the hallway draft.

Hope scribbled a final journal line:

Corporate Presidents/ Prophets hoard billions; my children hoard truth. Advantage: truth.

She lay beside Anna on the sofa, her arm forming a human rampart, and listened until dawn painted attic beams in hesitant gold.

Chapter 8

Pain Procedure

Friday - Markdown 3:38 a.m.

Leo 's nightmares evolved. The Shadow Man appeared. He hid amongst filing -cabinet towers that now lined the meeting - house corridor, each drawer stamped CORPORATION OF LIES. Leo swung his TRUTH sword, but the blade snapped, re-forging mid-air into a carpenter's square that flashed pure light, slicing one cabinet in two. Five more cabinets sprouted where one fell. The Shadow Man lingered. He woke gasping, relief washing over him as the carpenter 's square lingered in his memory, still glowing.

Hope's Journal – 4:45 a.m. Abduction Replay

Day 8 – Today marks the anniversary of when Corbin's attorney removed Jemma and Fowley from my warm protective arms. I still hear their jagged, high -pitched screams as I feel their small grasping fingers being pried away, as Corbin 's attorney disappears with them into an office, leaving me without them for the first time since I'd had Jemma; she was four years old. My world collapsed then.

Dad was gone. His pickup truck would never carry me or them home again. Yet I feel his presence during these late nights and early mornings.

I sift through court-sealed records—Corbin claimed I was an 'imminent flight risk.' Projection masquerades as prophecy. I write today's journal entry twice. The first is pure scribble; the second, admissible.

I'll attach both to my personal archive—one for the court and the Social Security number changes, one for my descendants, whether they hate me or not. I mark it in Emma's post-graduation paperwork with a personal letter to each child and begin duplicate files, in case she, Leo, or my other miracles ever want to read this legacy of lies to uncover their own truths when they are adults. I shift and remove the papers from Emma's files, leaving them for Nikki, Tom, Amy, and Paul.

I'm concerned about Leo and Sebastian. Leo is pulling away, and Sebastian seems to be taking on too much. They all have too much to handle for their ages. No, not just for their ages, but for anyone.

To-do list: request a certified copy of the removal order; subpoena Corbin's attorney for the hearing. Talk to Leo if he will let me.

Faith: low

Resolve: high

4:45 a.m. – Dawn Prep

Hope woke before her alarm, pulse pattering faster than the rain's memory on the tin roof. The farmhouse smelled of cooled pine and yesterday's popcorn. Surgery day. She slipped into sweatpants and a loose t-shirt, tucking her plush sky -blue robe under her arm —armor woven from unexpected kindness. In her pocket, the "I am complete in Him" card felt like contraband courage.

The kitchen light revealed Tom already there in cargo shorts, packing a soft-sided cooler. "Protein bars, vanilla collagen shake, sliced peaches, and one illicit doughnut for post-op victory," he said. "Van's nice and cool."

Emma padded in next, her hair braided tight, a Psalm card tucked behind her phone case. She set a thermos of herbal tea—ginger, no mint—on the counter. Hope raised an eyebrow; Emma grinned. "Not me—Nikki. She swears ginger wards off hospital germs and cures an upset stomach."

The twins thumped downstairs, mismatched shoes on wrong feet. Sebastian followed, a banner pole strapped like a lopsided lance. Anna appeared last, a lavender El Roi card pinned to her headband like a badge; she'd written WONDERFUL across it in glitter pen.

Hope's breath caught. "The banner stays here," she reminded. Sebastian propped it in the hallway, the crimson fabric glowing in the porch light.

5:00 a.m. – Van Blessing

Outside, dawn painted the clouds pearl-pink. Pastor Marcus waited by the van, Bible in hand. He read Psalm 121, his voice low so as not to fracture the dawn.

"The Lord shall preserve thy going out and thy coming in…"

Tom added sotto voce, "And unlike some prophets, our Beneficiary isn't listed at Delaware Trust."

Marcus cracked a grin; Hope caught the reference—

"Corporation of the President," shell after shell. Banner or balance sheet, pick one.

Her children circled Hope, laying hands on her shoulders—Matthew's sticky fingers, Molly's gentle palm, Leo's steady weight. Anna squeezed Hope's elbow. Emma whispered, "No weapon formed against you shall prosper, from Isaiah 54:17. Here, it's from Nikki," sliding a peach-colored card into her mother's palm.

Marcus anointed Hope's forehead with a dot of olive oil. "Surgeon's hands, steady; nerves, obedient; peace, prevailing." Hope blinked back tears she refused to shed.

6:00 a.m. – Route 95 Northbound

The van passed an exit sign for Warwick. Emma traced the arrow with her gaze.

"Is Gramps's house close to here?" she asked quietly.

Hope's throat pinched. "Just beyond that forestry sign. But remember—I deeded it to his and Grandma Amy and Grandpa Paul's church when they needed it for a family like ours. The place isn't safe for us anymore; Jim, Jemma, Fowley—they all know the address."

Tom glanced in the rearview mirror. "Safer at the Bridge House—hidden bridge, hidden home."

Hope nodded, forcing herself to watch the woods blur until the exit vanished.

6:45 a.m. – Check-in

The drive to Rhode Island was hushed, except for Sammy's commentary on sunrise colors. The hospital lot gleamed wet; Nikki double-parked momentarily to let the patient and her escorts out before parking the van and gathering reinforcements, Amy and Paul, to meet them inside with the younger, sleepier children.

Tom, Emma, and Sebastian escorted Hope into the lobby. Nurse Wendy— a warm-eyed woman with black hair woven with silver beads in her braids— met them, clipboard ready.

"Still ginger-freckled, Emma?" she teased, recognizing them from pre-op labs. Emma offered a shy nod.

Once everyone arrived, Wendy checked each ID band, then pressed a heart sticker to Anna's hand. "Prayer warriors get badges."

Behind the desk, a muted news chyron scrolled: **"LDS Investment Fund pays $5 million SEC fine."**

Emma read it and whispered, "Pocket change." Leo muttered, "Cost of closing a cabinet drawer."

Hope signed forms—consent, liability, living will copy. Wendy murmured, "We'll patch more than we poke." Hope exhaled gratitude.

The children clustered around their mother; Sebastian raised an imaginary banner over her shoulders.

Leo cleared his throat. "Mom, engine spark plugs fire when gaps are perfect. Nerves will do the same."

Hope smiled. Matthew recited *Yahweh-Yireh—God provides* like a spell. Molly added *Yahweh-Rapha—Healer* with her eyes squeezed shut. Sammy declared, "No weapon can pass by," his young voice squeaking. Matthew giggled. Molly shushed him.

Anna produced a folded Psalm 139 page. "Fearfully, wonderfully made," she whispered.

Hope's chest tightened, not with terror but with swollen affection. She gripped each hand. "See you on the other side. All is well. No worries."

Amy and Paul Gideon gathered beside the children with Nikki, holding a small sign that read "Livingston Banner Crew." Nurse Wendy greeted them and turned to Hope. "Hospital policy says minors stay with guardians. This lot looks trustworthy. Are you sure?"

Nurse Wendy cared for Hope before her marriage to Jim. This was the first time she noticed Hope's unforced smile since before that wedding.

Amy winked. "We've run tougher nurseries," she said, glancing at Hope, recalling Jemma and Fowley, tears caught in her throat.

Nurse Wendy spoke to Sebastian, her soulful brown eyes sparkling. "Keep Mom's banner flying till she's back, okay?" Then to Hope, her voice dropped: "I'll be speaking to folks on the highest floors—no patient of mine should face surgery under threat of life endangerment! These babes, too? This can't be right!" Her tone carried the authority backed by those above her badge.

Hope clung to her charge nurse's so- called "Cain's cursed colored hand." For over two decades Nurse Wendy had served as more than Hope 's liferaft during these nerve ablation procedures. Wendy kept her patient distracted with lighthearted and warm chatter, consistently helped Hope to ease through what others viewed as excruciatingly painful procedures. Hope saw in Wendy only light and kindness; no curse. Conflicting facts. Light skinned Mormons inflicted her injuries. Her nurse and doctors had pigmented skin.

Hope looked on as Emma handed over Sammy 's favorite plush lamb to Amy, and the children trooped behind their adoptive grandparents toward the cafeteria, leaving her with Nikki, Tom, and Wendy for pre -op check - in. Nikki and Tom soon followed the older Gideon couple, Amy, Paul, and Hope 's brood to the cafeteria. Wendy wheeled Hope through double doors, the familiar fluorescent corridor yawning like the future itself.

7:37 a.m. – Operating room

Dr. Sato, mask dangling, explained the ablation once more. Hope's gaze drifted to the ceiling tiles.

"I am beloved in Christ... Really? What Dr. Sato? Nurse Wendy?"

An orderly taped Jim's wedding ring inside a micro-envelope. She thought of her foolishness for wearing it and barely felt the IV start.

Dr. Sato squeezed Hope's hand. "You'll feel warmth, then nothing. You know the drill, Hope." They placed headphones with a soft melody featuring a woman's strong vocals—strangely familiar yet altogether different—It is Well with My Soul.

Hope's last waking thought: "Be still and know that I AM God."

8:04 a.m. – Waiting-room Watch

The surgical waiting area resembled every waiting room Hope had ever endured: pastel seascapes, vending machines that ate dollar bills, seats stitched in corporate mauve. Yet Tom and the kids transformed it into a fort. Sebastian unfolded banner posters into placemats atop two pushed-together tables; Nikki (arriving straight from the bakery) lined the edges with blueberry muffins. Pastor Marcus claimed a corner, scrolling Psalms on his tablet.

Emma paced near the window, phone buzzing again: Jim R.—Tick-tock. She slid it to airplane mode. Leo noticed her pale cheeks.

"You okay, Em?" he murmured.

"Just noise," she whispered. Leo's jaw flexed, but he nodded, opting for silence that wouldn't spook the twins.

Anna perched beside Molly, drawing a cartoon surgeon wielding a crimson banner instead of a scalpel. Sammy guarded the muffin tray, announcing, "No doughnut holes, but blueberry planets taste okay."

Grandma Amy scrolled her phone and shook her head.

"Salt Lake just opened another luxury mall—tithes at work."

Paul's voice was dry: "Render unto Caesar, then build Caesar a food court; forget starving members, much less strangers." Grandpa Paul then sucked in his cheeks and slumped in his chair. "Here ye! Here ye! I am but a poor, emaciated waif and faithful tithepayer, ignored by the blissfully aware self-paid LDS Presidents. Spare some change, Mr. President, Sir?!" Changing to a stern, old-sounding voice, reminiscent of a Modern Day LDS President, he answered his own question, "Why, no son, I don 't carry change. Why don't you try our Food Court? My wives both enjoy the Chinese food."

Grandma Amy couldn't help but giggle. "Paul! Stop—it's not funny!"

Tom emerged from a pay-phone alcove, wiping his hands on cargo shorts. "Radiator hose holding, by the way." The kids rolled their eyes; tension cracked like thin ice. Then the room erupted in laughter—everyone except Tom.

"Come on, what'd I say? Do I have toilet paper stuck to my shoe or something?" He looked down to check, and the laughter intensified.

The front desk joined in, laughing with them, and eventually, Tom laughed too. None of them seemed to know what they were laughing about.

Grandma Amy just had a contagious laugh.

9:22 a.m. – Status call

Nurse Wendy appeared, her mask lowered to reveal a reassuring smile. "Ablation underway, vitals steady. Doctor says textbook progress."

A collective exhale rippled through the room. Nikki offered a prayer, her voice hushed: "God our Banner Who wins all wars, we don't know what to do, so we lift our prayers and praises to You to win this Battle for Hope through her physicians and caregivers. Thank You for the source of Your Name, from Moses' arms uplifted and supported by others, so You would claim our victories. Yahweh Nissi, in our True Savior's name." Leo found himself amen-ing before he realized, along with the rest of the room.

10:03 a.m. – Glitch & grace

A vending machine swallowed Matthew's dollar with a metallic gulp. Tears threatened; Molly stomped. Tom jimmied the refund lever—nothing.

Pastor Marcus elbowed Nikki. She fished a roll of quarters from her purse and slipped it to Matthew. "Machines respect quarters more than singles."

He grinned, tension easing. The machine surrendered fruit snacks—Matthew's new evidence of providence.

Sebastian tapped his flow-chart sketch in progress.

"Even this vending machine posts profits to pay tax. LDS hides billions behind 'religious tax exemption.' Feels like wrong math for the wrong Savior."

Pastor Marcus replied, "In the Bible, my Jesus flipped tables for less."

Emma continued pacing, flipping through a blocked numbers list, DM haunting her memory. She typed a draft reply—Don't scare us—then deleted it. Better to starve trolls.

11:16 a.m. – Post-op news

Dr. Sato entered, wearing a disposable cap like a victory laurel. "Procedure successful. Ablated nerves cooled nicely. She's waking in recovery; pain should drop in half within a week."

Cheers punctured the waiting-room hush; even the vending machine seemed to hum along. Anna high-fived Molly so hard the smack echoed.

Dr. Sato added, gaze serious, "But rest matters. No heavy lifting—no undue physical or emotional tolls—rest is mandatory for forty-eight hours. Cool 15 minutes on, 15 off, but no heat, either. Hope knows the drill, but under the circumstances..."

Tom saluted. "We'll guard her from drama."

Emma's phone buzzed again—blocked number bypassing airplane mode with a voicemail ping. She ignored it, stomach tightening.

Noon – Recovery bay

Hope surfaced to the soft beeping of monitors and the hum of ceiling vents. Wendy's face hovered, a benevolent moon. "Back on earth, Ms. Livingston."

Pain hovered at a three instead of a nine. Hope licked her dry lips. "Kids?" "In safe orbit," Wendy smiled. "Family reunion in thirty."

Hope's fingers brushed the *accepted* card tucked under the blanket edge— someone had slipped it into her belongings bag. Tears pricked; anesthesia blurred them into a harmless prism.

12:47 p.m. – Reunion & wheelchair ride

The kids crowded around the reclining chair in pre-op Bay 3. Anna pressed the lavender El Roi badge to Hope's palm. "God saw you."

"Banner held," Sebastian added, lifting an imaginary pole. He offered a spark plug. "Trade for that IV?"

Hope chuckled—raw but real. Wendy supervised the transfer to a wheelchair. Nikki passed Tom the discharge paperwork; Tom skimmed and signed as "temporary guardian," a protective grin on his face.

Hope noticed Emma's forced smile, worry simmering beneath. Questions could wait until the pain meds wore thin.

2:30 p.m. – Homecoming ramen

The van bumped into the drive; rain-washed pines swayed overhead. Tom and Leo guided Hope to the sofa. Nikki started ramen—five packs, doctoring the broth with soy and a dash of lime. Leo insisted on stirring; steam fogged his glasses.

"Chef jokes beat nightmare fuel," he declared.

Hope managed half a bowl; the flavor tasted like college memories not yet poisoned by fear. The twins slurped; Sammy arranged noodles into banner shapes.

Anna fetched extra pillows, her shy caretaking emerging like dawn after a storm.

markdown 5:10 p.m. – Sebastian tithing-flow flow-chart

Sebastian spread poster board across the coffee table while Hope dozed. One column was labeled **ENGINE FUEL**, the other **CHURCH MONEY**.

Arrows traced:

spark-plug → combustion → motion;

parallel arrows traced

10% income → LDS investment arm → 100B corpus → commercial real estate.

He titled it, **"Why My Mom's Van Runs on Gas, But God's Work Runs on Gold?"**

Pastor Reuben, dropping off photocopies, blinked at the chart and whispered,

"That'll preach, kid."

7:05 p.m. – Sunset hush

Pain meds thinned; Hope dozed while the children played quiet banner charades. Emma finally confessed to Nikki in the kitchen: "Jim DM'd threats about the courts."

Nikki frowned. "Show your mom?"

"Not yet—surgery day." Emma's voice cracked. Nikki squeezed her shoulder. "We'll loop Tom and Pastor Marcus, document everything."

Emma exhaled relief; sharing the threat halved its weight.

10:12 p.m. – Sebastian's spark-plug vow

Rain restarted, softer. Sebastian lingered in the hallway door, spark plug warm in his palm. Tom's breathing trick steadied him.

He whispered toward Hope—sleep-soft on the sofa— "Spark firing right, Mom. No worries tonight."

Hope, half-awake, murmured, "Grounded engines run far." Sebastian slipped upstairs, heart lighter than he could remember.

3:00 a.m. – Meds wore off Journal Entry

If billion-dollar prophets and their passed-down olive oil can't heal my spine, I'll trust the Carpenter who still works for free. Thank You, Yeshua Messiah, El Roi, Jehovah Rapha, Jehovah Jireh, and You with Sacred Nams I do not know, in my beloved Savior's name. I can no longer bear to hear or speak or write about You in English, because minding my Priesthood has turned my spark plug rusty. I will learn to praise Your Sacred Names in the language that You used, my true Messiah, my Lord, my God. Thank you!

Hope climbed off the sofa and began wading through the legal files and medical records of her past, finding and marking patterns as she sewed the tapestry of her forgotten memories of who she used to be and what had happened to her — together.

Chapter 9

Summons & Shields

Saturday, 7:30 a.m. – 2:30 p.m.

7:15 a.m. – Envelope of thunder

Hope sat at the pine table, a legal packet shimmering under the single Edison bulb. The house smelled of instant coffee and damp cedar. Amy hovered by the stove, pouring hot water over chicory grounds. Tom leaned against the doorway, arms folded like a rampart. The children were still upstairs, muffled laughter rising with the oscillating fan—safe for the moment.

She slit the pouch. **Petition for Emergency Modification of Custody** screamed in bold. Jim's attorney cousin argued that Hope's "transient residence" and "unstable mental condition post-surgery" endangered the children. Hearing set in thirteen days.

Hope's pulse skipped. "He's pushing fast."

Tom read over her shoulder, jaw tightening. "Emergency modifications break if you show stable shelter."

"But a safe-house address can't go on record," Amy said, her voice trembling.

Tom growled, "Funny—Salt Lake manages to hide $100 billion behind a single 'Corporation Sole' address and nobody blinks."

Hope pressed her fingertips to her forehead and then to her mid spine —the surgery incision throbbed. *No heavy emotional lifting*, Dr. Sato had warned. Hope remembered. Too late.

8:02 a.m. – Elders converge

A knock: Pastors Ruben and Marcus flanked by Elder Chavez with a battered laptop bag and Elder Harper cradling a box of security cameras. "Shields," Marcus announced, stepping inside. "Physical, digital, and legal."

Hope's smile looked tired, as she welcomed them into the Safe House. Harper set the cameras on the table. "These run cellular—no internet trail. We'll cover the porch and drive."

Chavez opened the laptop — a refurbished tower, monitor, ergonomic keyboard—and arranged them neatly. A sticky note on the lid read: "SEC v. Ensign Peak, $5 million fine—proof even prophets file late when profits loom large."

Sebastian mouthed "five million" as if it were science fiction.

Chavez motioned to Hope and explained, "Talk and it types. Less strain on you. More words may flow with time. No licensing either; the fee is skimmed off tithes."

Hope whispered thanks, her throat tight. Chavez handed Tom a thumb drive. "Secure call app to reach a Christian family -law firm we trust. No cousin overlap."

Tom pocketed it like a cartridge.

Marcus unfolded an envelope from his Bible. "The ARC benevolence fund will cover the initial retainer. We anticipated your husband's letter."

Hope's vision blurred. Gifts again—this time shields, not confusing Mormon casseroles. Hope began, "I don't know how to repay—"

"Family doesn't invoice," Marcus echoed Tom 's earlier line. He placed a hand over the custody papers, then over Psalm 139 still taped nearby. "One blood, one banner."

10:20 a.m. – Camera crew & curious kids

Electric drills whined as Chavez and Tom mounted cameras under the eaves. Sebastian fetched screws, relishing his foreman status. Matthew and Molly argued whether the cameras counted as "angel eyes" or "robot raccoons."

Anna, still in pajamas, dictated Psalm 139 into the new computer. The dictation software misheard "wonderfully" as "wander fully"; she giggled and corrected it, courage rising with each line.

Leo lugged the ladder, cracking a joke about "Heavenly surveillance" but casting wary glances toward the driveway — echoes of nightmares not far behind.

Hope, seated on the sofa, winced at incision twinges but forced slow breaths. Watching the tech shields rise steadied her heartbeat more than pain meds.

11:35 a.m. – Secure counsel call

Hope skimmed the petition again; a side note from Jim's cousin cited "spiritual welfare" under IRS § 508(c)(1)(A).

Amy snorted. "Translation: tax shelter with a hymnbook cover."

Tom plugged the thumb drive into the laptop, launching a green -shield icon. Marcus paired Bluetooth earbuds to Hope 's phone and dialed. A calm female voice answered: "Mason & Greenway Family Law, Confidential Line

Hope introduced herself, her voice trembling. Attorney Greenway requested details; Amy read bullet points from the petition. Hope described safe -house protocols, surgery recovery, and Jim's history. The attorney's responses were crisp: "Emergency order challengeable. We'll file opposition Monday. The court can hold the sealed address. And we'll remind the judge that a church that moves $100 billion through Delaware LLCs can certainly afford supervised visitation for one of their top constituents," Greenway added.

Hope's shoulders sagged—not from defeat but relief.

Greenway concluded, "Document every threat—screenshots, voicemails. Breathe; we fight this in daylight, not shadows."

Hope removed the earbuds, tears slipping free. Marcus handed her a linen handkerchief embroidered with a cross—edges softened from decades of pocket prayers.

12:50 p.m. – Banner lunch drill

Nikki arrived with sub sandwiches and sparkling water. The kids formed a line, Sebastian announcing "Operation Feed Fortress." Anna taped her El Roi badge to the computer monitor. "God sees us typing."

Napkins bore printed verse Acts 17:26; Molly colored hearts around *one blood*. Matthew demanded extra mustard "for unity."

Leo flashed his phone—headline read,

"Wall Street Journal: "LDS Tithes Fund Real-Estate Empire." He shook his head. "Jesus flipped tables for less square footage." Nikki replied, "So we keep flipping pages—Scripture, not shares."

Hope swallowed turkey, realizing her taste had returned—fear hadn't eclipsed her hunger.

Nikki caught Emma pocketing her phone with practiced stealth. "DM again?"

Emma nodded, her eyes glassy. Nikki guided her to the porch steps. "Document, don't dialogue."

Emma forwarded voicemails to the new legal-evidence folder Chavez set up. Each send felt like dropping heavy stones.

2:05 p.m. – Quiet after storm

Cameras blinked green. The laptop fan hummed. Kids sprawled on quilts, watching a DVD of VeggieTales: Gideon the Tuba Warrior—no internet required.

Sebastian slid his flow-chart draft under Hope's hand:

arrows linking **"Member Tithes→ Ensign Peak Advisors→ Shopping Malls & Stocks"**

Hope traced the lines, whispering, "Truth in crayons outshouts lies in boardrooms."

Leo dozed upright, clutching a spark plug like a talisman; the nightmare ambience retreated behind his eyelids.

Marcus and the elders departed, promising to check in on Sunday. Nikki left a fresh loaf of zucchini bread on the counter— "armor for midnight snack attacks."

Hope leaned against the fridge, stitches aching but her heart bolstered by shields. The legal packet lay beside Psalm 139—ugly words restrained by beautiful truth.

She mused, "If courts confuse CEOs with prophets, we'll subpoena the ledger and let the Carpenter testify."

She whispered to the kitchen's hum: "Banner stands."

9:30 p.m. – How Protective Are Protective Orders?

Mandrake forwarded a study:

63% of protective orders are violated within the first year. I didn't need the statistic; I have voicemail evidence.

I draft a brief on interstate enforcement gaps— Utah to Oregon relay failed, California served late. Highlight the timeline. Judges love timelines.

Pain today: wrists inflamed. Brace both hands; type with my thumbs. I feel ridiculous, but ridiculous still files motions.

Evening: neighborhood kids set off fireworks for a church rally. Downstairs and alone, I hit the floor, my heart sprinting until my brain caught up. I just hurt my back and neck. Fireworks are not pipe bombs.

Add note: proximity triggers.

Maybe the court and Social Security will understand detonations if I outline them in DSM and medical terms. Will Dr. Sato testify?

Chapter 10

Court Countdown

Monday, 8:45 a.m. – 3:40 p.m.
8:45 a.m. – Video consult

Hope blinked at the refurbished monitor—freshly anchored atop the pine table. Elder Chavez's dictation software mic captured her nervous breaths as Attorney Lydia Greenway's face filled the screen: a neat bun, tortoise-shell glasses, voice crisp like a fresh apple bite.

"Thirteen-day runway," Greenway began. "Our opposition filing goes out today;" She added, "We'll also remind the court that Jim's tithing affidavits list his payments to 'The Corporation of the President,' not to any registered church. A charity that signs contracts as a 'Corporation Sole' is admitting it runs on profit law, not Pauline letters."

Tom muttered, "Caesar with a hymnbook."

Greenway continued, "The judge will weigh the sealed-address request tomorrow. I'll need sworn statements: documented surgeries, safe-house admission, Jim's history of abandonment, if any."

Hope's incision throbbed. "Records from Corbin's case are in a storage tote in the kitchen—box labels only I understand. I've begun cross-referencing them inside the documents to show patterns." She glanced at the children building a banner rack out of earshot in the backyard.

Greenway's gaze softened. "Unearth what you can. Every missing tooth in Jim's custody smile helps us."

Hope nodded. A memory flashed—hospital wristband dated *November 2009*, Corbin's name scrawled as emergency contact. She flagged it mentally. **[RF1]**

"Final note," Greenway added. "Ignore direct threats; forward them. Stalkers thrive on engagement."

Hope exhaled. "No responses. Just evidence."

10:05 a.m. – DIY banner rack

Tom spread two-by-four rails and angle brackets on the lawn. Leo wielded a cordless drill, channeling temple-corridor energy into pilot holes. Sebastian measured twice, crowding like a structural engineer. Matthew and Molly fetched screws from a beach pail repurposed as a hardware bucket.

"Banner mast slides here," Tom explained, tapping guide holes. Anna sat cross-legged nearby, scribbling *EL ROI* in bubble letters on the rack's base.

Sebastian tapped the two-by-four. "If boards were dollars, the Latter-Day Saints' Jesus, who owns the Corporations in Ensign Peak, they could build a bridge to the moon."

Leo snorted. "Yeah—but they'd still charge admission. And I have a feeling their Jesus would only sell one-way tickets to people like us."

Hope watched from the porch rocker, laptop balanced on her knees. Dictation software transcribed her murmured dates:

"June 2012—nerve ablation lumbar, August 2012 ganglion impar block, October 2012 thoracic steroid injection, December 2012 ganglion impar block, February, April, July, October 2013 ganglion impar block, February 2014—nerve ablation lumbar; more ganglion impar nerve blocks then in August 2014—scheduled C-section twins." Words appeared as if she had softly typed them fluidly, like unspooling ghost tape.

Emma paced with the garden hose, cooling drilling sparks. She nudged Hope' s shoulder. "He DM'd again last night—just the word tick. I forwarded."

Hope flinched but kept her gaze steady. "Attorney has it. No oxygen for shadows. Em, Attorney Greenway seems to understand." Emma nodded.

11:42 a.m. – Grace paradox

Banner rack erected, crimson cloth flapped under the noonday sun — victorious scarecrow. Children sprawled in the shade, sipping watered-down lemonade. Anna sidled beside Hope, El Roi card fluttering like a reluctant moth.

"Mom," she began, drawing invisible circles on the porch slat, "if God sees everything... does He love Jim too?"

The question landed like a pebble in Hope 's post-surgery chest. Behind the spreadsheet window lurked a PDF Amy had forwarded with Greenway 's thread:

***IRS Form 990-T — LDS Deseret Management Corporation*, proof that even prophets file business returns.**

Greenway held up Exhibit B: the KSL -TV studios parcel map and FCC license registry, naming Deseret Management as sole owner. "They control the message from the transmitter to the pulpit," she added.

Hope clicked it shut; the poisonous truth documented but not ingested. She closed the laptop, her mind racing through Latter -Day Saint doctrine and promised curses versus the comfort she found in the Bible itself. The curse of Eternal Damnation just for asking a question was her starting point. Too many questions to even form, much less ask.

Before she could respond, Sebastian spoke from the steps, wiping sawdust off his tee. "Tom says spark plugs don't check a driver's character; they just fire when grounded. Maybe love's like that." He shrugged, surprised by his own analogy.

Hope inhaled. "Love isn't approval, sweatheart. God can love your dad while hating what he does. Like a doctor loving a patient while cutting out poison. And you only get one earthly dad. Grace wins, make sense?"

Anna mulled it over, nodding slowly. "So we pray Jim, er Dad, gets the poison out? Or that God does?"

"We pray truth finds him," Hope amended, astonished by her own words. Grace tasted strange—sweet with an after-kick.

12:30 p.m. – Sandwich strategy

Amy delivered turkey-cheddar sliders; Pastor Marcus arrived with a satchel of legal- size envelopes. He pulled Hope aside. "The judge scheduled the first tele - conference for Friday. Greenway will speak; you may listen muted."

Hope's pulse quickened. "Friday—will the banner stay here?"

Marcus chuckled. "One blood flows through Wi-Fi too." He handed Emma a packet labeled *EVIDENCE LOG*. "Document chain."

Emma tucked it under her sunflower tee, now a newly minted paralegal.

2: 05 p.m. – Memory box dig

Leo and Sebastian carried in another storage tote from the van's rear hatch. Dust motes swirled as Hope cracked the lid. Hospital billing statements rustled like brittle leaves. She lifted a file: Corbin v. Livingston Protective

Order, 2009. The margins bore Corbin 's handwritten note — She overreacted. Hope 's hands trembled; dictation software captured a whisper:

"Forced epidural after assault; nerve damage flare." **[RF2]**

Anna gently placed the file on the scanner bed Tom rigged from a thrift-store flatbed. Each beep felt like a nail driven into Jim's emergency petition.

3:10 p.m. – Van break & confession ripple

Tom called Leo to the driveway—radiator coolant top-off lesson. Over hood steam, Leo finally voiced the shadowy figure of a not-so-stranger in full. Tom listened, adjusting the radiator cap.

"You named what's eating you," Tom said. "Now you eat at it. Next nightmare, picture an exit sign shaped like your spark plug, and ask the shadow to show his face. You have a safety exit."

Leo exhaled, feeling lighter. Inside, Hope saw the exchange through the kitchen window—her son's shoulders no longer hunched.

3:40 p.m. – Segment pause & looming request

Phone buzzed: voicemail transcription from the Maine District Court Clerk—Jim's attorney filed an emergency visitation request for supervised contact next week. Marcus read it, jaw set: "A new front opens."

Emma opened the court-clerk PDF: filing fee stamped

"PAID BY THE CORPORATION OF THE PRESIDENT, LDS CHURCH"

Even the threat carried a corporate watermark.

Hope steadied herself on the banner rack rail. Storms kept testing stakes, but the wood felt solid, crimson fabric catching late-afternoon light like promise.

Monday 6:15 p.m. – 11:58 p.m.
6:15 p.m. – Strategy Zoom

The farmhouse glowed with lamp warmth as Attorney Greenway's face reappeared on the monitor. Hope perched carefully on the edge of her chair to avoid straining her surgical wound; EVIDENCE LOG open while Amy, Paul, Tom, and Nikki filled the frame edges like sentries. Kids clustered upstairs, brushing teeth and taking showers, with Emma on bedtime routine early patrol shift.

Greenway summarized: "We've filed to quash Jim's emergency visitation request—grounds: intimidation, stalking photo, prior abuse orders. The judge orders a telephone status conference Friday at 9 a.m. Your presence muted, Ms. Livingston, reinforces transparency."

Hope nodded, stitches aching. "What about the sealed address?"

"Judge granted a preliminary seal pending inspection. Clerks will reference Bridge House as P.O. Box for an ARC church only." Relief sputtered through the room like generator ignition.

Greenway continued. "Your 2009 protective-order scans are gold. Corbin's handwritten 'She overreacted' note frames credibility issues." She raised a brow. "Any more hospital records proving long-term injury?" Hope tapped the tote—yes, more to scan tonight.

"One more thing," Greenway said. "Send me the SEC whistleblower article you bookmarked last night. Judges respect timelines, and the $100 billion deception sets context for Jim's sudden 'financial concern' for the children."

Leo whispered to Sebastian, "Mom's evidence beats Latter-Day Saint spin-doctor heads." Sebastian doodled "Ugly & Fake" under the Latter-Day Saint spin column—kids processing warfare in cartoons.

7:40 p.m. – Supper & civil courage

Dinner was zucchini-bread French toast, Marcus' impromptu recipe. Matthew declared it "banner fuel." Molly renamed syrup "shield oil."

During bites, Hope asked Greenway one last question: "What if Jim shows up at the Safe House?"

Greenway's voice turned steel. "Call 911, cite the sealed order. Document everything, disengage. Your cameras are our silent witnesses."

Hope relayed Greenway's unwavering message to the others. Each one nodded solemnly—battle briefing absorbed.

Natural Child ESTRANGEMENT by an Abusive Parent Does NOT = Child Alienation

Estrangement = natural recoil when a child has been or witnessed abuse upon the non-offending parent

Alienation = unnatural distancing by a child who mirrors and parrots the offending parent's complaints about the non-abusive parent

Hope dictated these words, cut them out, highlighted them in orange, and taped them to the laptop screen, out of sight of her own children.

8:55 p.m. – Late-night research rabbit hole

The house quieted; Nikki and Amy drove home. Hope settled at the computer with ginger tea, Dictation software mic active. She did a web search for "LDS SEC whistleblower tithing billions." An article surfaced about the $5 billion fine—Hope read aloud; Dictation software transcribed. [RF3]

She clicked another link— **"LDS shell companies & political donations."** Her pulse quickened. The doctrine Joseph Smith built felt less sacred, more like governmental and corporate scaffolding entwined.

She bookmarked **God Loves Mormons** videos for tomorrow's daylight viewing—nights belonged to nerves and ablation scars. Yet truth breadcrumbs laid a trail forward.

10:03 p.m. – Anna's lantern

Anna tiptoed into the glow. "Mom, the laptop light leaks into the hallway—Sammy thinks it's ghosts."

Hope dimmed the brightness. "Just ghosts of old doctrine."

Anna climbed onto the sofa, holding a Psalm 139 printout now covered in glitter star stickers. "Stars crack and jiggle," she recited, paraphrasing Hope's earlier reassurance. Hope kissed her curls. "Art does, sweetheart."

11:12 p.m. – Leo's spark-plug mantra

Across the hall, Leo rehearsed Tom's nightmare counter: he pictured an EXIT sign shaped like a spark plug and mouthed, "SHOW YOUR FACE!" to the shadow to come. He whispered "gap perfect, ground steady" until his eyelids surrendered. The corridor dream flickered but could not fully ignite.

11:58 p.m. – Headlight scare

A camera chime split the silence. Hope's heart lurched; she clicked the live feed. Headlights idled at the far end of the gravel lane, just beyond motion range—an eerie glow among the pines. The vehicle sat for thirty seconds, then turned and reversed, red taillights vanishing down the county road.

Hope saved the clip to **EVIDENCE LOG**. She inhaled through her nose, hissing out through her mouth; Tom 's breathing trick. The banner cloth rustled in the hallway draft—a reminder that poles and prayers held.

She hand penned a journal line:

Headlights prowl but the light inside is stronger. Friday court call ahead. Engines grounding, stars watching.

Chapter 11

Leo's Lingering Night Terrors & Homework

Hope's Journal: Mortgage Bribes and Hallway Footfalls

7:55 a.m. Power hiccups; the fridge wheezes like an asthmatic deacon. The ensuing silence is sermon enough: pay or perish. Yesterday's mail contained three cashier's checks Mother sent to Bullock's Mortgage —five payments ahead to the Judge who decided Jemma and Fowley's custodial fate. Memo lines blank, silence purchased in looping **B** cursive. I scan at G00 dpi; each pixel of hush becomes Exhibit H-2.

Night report: 2:17 a.m. hallway creak. I shuffled out expecting plumbing ghosts but found Leo flat-footed, workshop light haloing his silhouette. He whispered in his sleep, "It's nothing, Mom," eyes wild, before slipping back into the boys' room. Sleepwalking again. The scent of soldier and fear clung to his hoodie. I logged the incident, date-stamped and unsigned, afraid a signature would make whatever happened to him prophetic. He needs help bigger than Tom. I'll call when the phone lines open.

Tuesday, 8:15 a.m. – 4:45 p.m.

8:15 a.m. – Homeschool launch

Morning sunlight ricocheted off the refurbished monitor as Hope wrote *BANNER ACADEMY – DAY 1* on a sheet of butcher paper taped to the fridge. The pine table transformed into a classroom: spiral notebooks, colored pens, and a stack of scripture printouts—KJV on white, Book of Mormon passages highlighted on canary yellow.

Sebastian rang a thrift-store desk bell. "Class, please turn to Acts 17:26."

Matthew saluted; Molly performed an exaggerated curtsey. Sammy, assigned "Tech Captain," clicked open a PowerPoint slide titled **ONE BLOOD vs MANY CURSES**.

Leo shifted at the end, history textbook open but gaze drifting to the window where Tom's Honda idled—garage shift beckoning. He fingered yesterday's pay stub in his pocket: $45 cash—spark-plug install & brake drum sanding. His first paycheck ever. Sebastian worked for free.

Anna adjusted her lavender El Roi headband—new glitter star added. She whispered to Emma, "Ready?"

Hope, still sore from surgery, sat nearby as facilitator, Dictation software mic on to transcribe the lecture for records. "Begin with Acts."

8:40 a.m. – Class rebellion

Emma read Acts 17:26 Molly underlined *one blood*. Anna then stood, her voice trembling at first but growing: "Now read yellow 2 Nephi 5:21." Sebastian projected it on the screen.

Molly's jaw tightened; Matthew muttered, "Ugly spark."

"Today's experiment," Anna announced, "is to count contradictions." She distributed sticky notes labeled *truth spark* and *lie spark*.

Hope froze—this wasn't her planned lesson. Yet Anna wielded courage like the banner itself. The twins plastered lie-spark notes all over 2 Nephi, giggling as the yellow page vanished under neon.

When Sammy stuck a lie-spark to the video camera lens, Hope burst into laughter—painful but liberating. Hope would prepare a citation lesson in English and let the children write research paragraphs.

10:05 a.m. – Phone buzz with new legal twist

Hope's cell pinged: an email from Richardson & Price CC'd to Greenway. "Request for immediate on-site evaluation of minors' living conditions. Proposed date: this Thursday."

Two days. Hope 's stomach clenched; her incision still throbbed from her firework freefall. She forwarded it to Greenway. Almost instantly, Greenway replied: "We'll oppose— insufficient notice, sealed address. Deep breaths."

Hope inhaled Tom's garage trick, exhaled a Psalm. "Yehova Jireh, Yehova Nissa, Yeshua, My Messiah, thank you for being the God Who Is always with me and these children in my care! I claim the stripes and mind of my Savior! I worship You! In the true Savior's name," Hope whispered in awe and defiant praise—more for her seven miraculous children than for herself.

10:45 a.m. – Leo heads to the shop

Tom honked twice—prearranged signal. Leo grabbed the spark-plug keychain Tom had printed on a 3-D printer. Before leaving, he touched Hope 's shoulder. "Class war looks fun. I'll fight Latter -Day -Saint -Spin-Doctor brakes."

Hope squeezed his hand. "Be back for school soon, apprentice."

He strode out, shoulders squared—nightmare corridor shrinking in the rearview.

12:30 p.m. – Lunch & IRS bombshell

Hope warmed leftover zucchini -bread French toast as the kids debated whether Moses homeschooled in the wilderness. Emma refreshed her news feed. An article headline popped: **"SEC Fines LDS Investment Arm for hiding $50 billion for Secret Ensign Funds."**

She gasped and read aloud. Anna's mouth formed a perfect O. "Fifty billion with a B?"

Hope bookmarked it, noting [RF3] research flag. The kids peppered her with questions— "How can a church hide billions?" "What does any church need with five billion dollars, much less fifty? Didn't the last article say 100 billion?" "Why was their fine only five million with an M and not with a B?" "Does that break tithing rules?" "Do they pay taxes on that like we do?" Hope promised an in-depth, student-directed research session tomorrow.

1:45 p.m. – Banner rack reinforcement

Sebastian drilled cross-braces to the banner stand, citing Proverbs 24:3— *"By wisdom a house is built."* Matthew measured degrees of wobble with a protractor app; Molly labeled each brace with a Hebrew name sticker. Anna painted purple stars on the base—her signature— with an Identity phrase.

Hope scanned another medical file, then glanced at the yellow pad. Her surgery debt—$38,000 still owed—looked microscopic beside LD$ Apple shares bought with widows ' mites. Dictation software captured her murmur: "Megachurch with a brokerage account; hijacked bride of Christ."

3:30 p.m. – Garage triumph

Leo returned, grease -smudged grin wider than the driveway. He handed Hope a crisp twenty and folded five — Tom insisted he keep the rest. "Changed oil like a champ. Tom says I gap plugs better than the manual."

Hope hugged him carefully. "Spark master."

Leo's eyes shone—his identity shifting from comedian shield to competent apprentice.

Hope knew his grades were slipping. The Lord provided an appointment with trauma neuropsychologist, Dr. Sung Li, in a few days for an evaluation. Self-pay was better than no care. Pastor Marcus had begun to pass the plate. Hope fought back tears of gratitude and worry for her children.

3:45 p.m. – DM flare & shield response

Emma 's phone vibrated: **Jim R.— "Tick tock, courts moving fast. You need to choose or I will choose for you. Who will it be? Marsi or your mom?"** She screenshot, forwarded to EVIDENCE LOG, then blocked the new number. No engagement. Latter-Day-Saint-Spin-Doctor gears snipped.

Pastor Marcus texted: **"Judge upheld sealed address. Visitation request postponed to formal hearing."** A collective exhale swept through the kitchen.

4:45 p.m. – Pings and Crimson Folds

Mosquito-laden dusk settled. A security camera pinged: the same headlights paused at the lane mouth—closer this time—then retreated. Chavez checked camera playback: a grainy silhouette leaning out the window, snapping a blurred photo of the license plate through his zoom lens.

Hope watched the clip loop, her heart steady but furious. Nikki stepped beside her, a lavender card glowing in the monitor light.

"God sees him, too," she said.

Hope nodded. "And cameras." She saved the clip as **Latter-Day-Saint-Spin_doctor_gears_003.mp4.**

The banner cloth rustled in the hallway, crimson against the gathering night.

6:05 p.m. – Legal shield upgrade

Hope, Tom, Nikki, and Pastor Marcus crowded around the monitor while Attorney Greenway replayed **Latter-Day-Saint-Spin_gears_003.mp4**.

Headlights haloed the banner rack; a silhouetted figure raised a phone, flash popping once before the car reversed.

Greenway's brows knit. "This meets stalking criteria. I'll file an addendum to the existing protective order—includes a no-photography clause and a 500- foot perimeter."

Tom asked, "Can we move another camera to catch plates next time?"

Chavez nodded via split screen, already scribbling a diagram. "Infrared lens in my trunk—installation tomorrow."

Hope exhaled. Every new shield felt like solder on cracked armor.

6:42 p.m. – Banner Manual workshop

Hope photographed the pad, saved it to the Doctrine Discrepancies folder, and muttered, "A corporation of the president indeed—PAID BY THE CORPORATION OF THE PRESIDENT, LDS CHURCH shows up on

every deed." Anna whispered, "Butter-toast religion—looks edible, feeds only itself." The phrase earned a sticky note in Banner Manual Section 2: **FALSE GODS THAT EAT TITHES.**

Dinner plates scraped clean as the kids commandeered the pine table for publishing. Sebastian folded construction paper into booklet form, titling it **BANNER MANUAL – VOLUME 1** in bold Sharpie.

Section 1: Hebrew Names—Molly glued stickers of Yahweh-Rapha: The Healer God beside bandaid doodles.

Section 2: Truth Sparks—Matthew listed contradictions they'd crushed, illustrating each Nephi, and verse lies spark with a cartoon dynamite stick.

Section 3: Stars & Bodies—Anna copied Psalm 139, embellishing with glitter constellations around the words wonderfully made.

Section 4: Follow the Finances

Sammy dictated his "angel-egg" parable to Dictation software: "Deviled eggs are just angel eggs wearing spicy coats. God sees the angel even with the spice." Dictation software transcribed "spicy goats," causing riotous laughter. Emma corrected it, a sticky-note laughing emoji affixed.

Hope watched, her heart swelling. Trauma therapy in Crayola packaging.

8:15 p.m. – Evening porch huddle

Nikki arrived with a plate of chocolate -chip scones— "victory biscuits." She, Amy, and Hope rocked on the porch as twilight deepened. Insects droned, and the banner rack stood silhouetted against the indigo sky.

Amy whispered, "Headlights or not, the banner is still visible."

Hope sipped ginger tea, her incision aching less tonight. "Visibility used to terrify me."

Nikki smiled. "Now it testifies."

9:50 p.m. – Research rabbit-hole II

With the kids tucked in, Hope returned to her glowing monitor, the dictation software mic poised. She opened a PDF of the SEC whistle-blower report: Latter -Day -Saint -Leaders ' hoard and hide billions in shell corporations. The article referenced "purely for the Second Coming fund."

Hope read aloud, dictation software recording:

"Church amassed $100 billion; when asked why, the presiding bishopric cited preparation for their jesus christ's millennial reign." [RF4]

A memory flared —Corbin quoting a bishop: *"Tithing secures celestial stock options."* She recalled Corbin telling her that he needed to forge signatures on donation slips to impress ward leadership. Shame pricked; she noted it for her attorney—proof of a violent, coercive finance culture.

10:28 p.m. – Flash memory: Corbin settlement

Digging deeper, she found 2011 settlement records: Corbin v. Company Safety—$25,000 for a back injury after a forklift mishap; where he wasn't the injured party. Corbin pocketed the payout She murmured, "Now I have the physical disabilities, forced into debt, gaslighting feels like mental strangulation." The dictation software captured every word.

Tears threatened; she paused to breathe. [**RF5**]

11:03 p.m. – Banner Manual debut

Sebastian descended in pajamas, clutching the freshly stapled *Banner Manual*. He handed it to Hope. "We'll add chapters with each victory."

Hope flipped through the pages—crayon theology and sticky-note footnotes, an angel-egg parable scrawled beside a smiling yolk. She stifled a soft laugh. "Canonical in my book."

He tapped an empty page labeled Chapter 10: Court Triumph. "Space reserved."

Hope ruffled his hair. "Faith fuel."

11:55 p.m. – Court notice ping

An email alert flashed: **Maine District Court**. Hope's pulse spiked as she clicked.

Tele-conference, Friday 9:00 a.m. Parties present by phone. Petitioner (Jim Richardson) granted live audio participation.

Jim's voice would pulse through the speakerphone, breaching safe walls with sound waves alone. Hope's hand trembled. She forwarded it to Greenway, tagged URGENT.

Greenway responded within minutes: *"Standard. We'll mute his direct address. You stay silent. Breathe."*

Hope breathed—count of four. The banner cloth rustled faintly in the hallway, as if responding.

12:17 a.m. – Journal entries

"Latter-Day-Saint-Spin eyes flash cameras, but light replicates. Banner Manual born—crayon creed.

SEC billions = empire façade; IRS fine feels prophetic. Jim's voice coming Friday.

I will mute my fear; the banner will speak."

3:03 a.m.

"I dream I'm folding Dad's funeral flag, and every crease skims my palms. Awake, my hands tingle with phantom burns. I press them to the window and watch Orion limp across the sky—the hunter missing a star, like me missing a father.

Greenway says causation is hard to prove—no medical examiner lists "courtroom humiliation" as a cause of death. I draft the victim-impact paragraph anyway: "On June 5, 2005, Applicant's father collapsed outside Courtroom 3B moments after the Defendant mocked his daughter's broken neck." Truth deserves an affidavit even if it never sees daylight.

Tonight, I feel the bend in my vertebrae like braille spelling useless. I read it until dawn."

She closed the notebook. Outside, the night was star-punctured silk. Inside, the children's banner rack gleamed—crimson stretching into tomorrow.

Chapter 12

Muted Voices, Louder Truths

Wednesday, 7:05 a.m. – 3:15 p.m.

7:05 a.m. – AC salvation & homeschool stir

Pastor Marcus's pickup rattled into the drive, a refurbished window unit strapped in the bed like captured prey. Amy waved from the passenger seat, brandishing a tray of egg-and-cheese biscuits. The cool morning air still clung to dew-wet pines, but forecasts screamed ninety-eight by noon.

Tom hoisted the AC through the living-room window while Leo and Sebastian sealed gaps with pool-noodle insulation. When the compressor kicked on, frosty breath puffed from the vents. Molly shrieked "Cloud machine!" and stuck her face in the airflow.

Hope, her incision easing, declared a half-day homeschool: "Science experiment—condensation on coils." The twins drew smiley droplets on poster board.

But Emma requested an add-on. She'd queued a short clip about the Book-of-Abraham papyri controversy—ARC's youth leader had supplied it. Hope allowed the screening, dictation software ready.

The video played: facsimiles mis-translated, Egyptologists' verdict. Matthew raised a hand. "If Joseph Smith was wrong on papyri from the Egyptian burial tomb, he might be wrong about Nephi's skin too." Sticky-note lie sparks slapped onto the manual chapter draft. Anna whispered, "Greek Mythology Latter-Day-Saint-Spin-Doctor-dragon heads keep popping up! Every time one is chopped down, more just sprout out in its place!"

Hope watched her children dismantle doctrine like Lego sets, her heart both proud and raw.

9:40 a.m. – Tom's phone-presence coaching

In the cooling living room, Tom set up a mock conference call. Hope held a spoon as a "mute button." Tom played Jim, his voice drawling threats. Hope practiced silent breathing, pressing the imaginary mute.

"Focus on fixed points," Tom advised. "Banner cloth, spark plug, Psalm card—anchor your senses."

Hope chose the spark-plug gap image: precise, grounded. Practice rounds thinned her dread to a manageable tremor.

11:10 a.m. – Legal letter drafting

Dictation software transcribed as Hope dictated a declaration to Greenway: details of stalking headlights, Jim's decades of financial neglect, Corbin's injury timeline ([RF5]). Marcus notarized the pages; Amy scanned them into the EVIDENCE LOG.

Emma added new DM screenshots; the folder grew like a digital fortress.

"Hang on," Emma said, opening a second tab. "Gramps's old ledger starts in 1993—he listed ZCMI, Beneficial Life, Deseret Cattle, a copper mine, and five Salt Lake office towers." She scrolled through newer filings on sabe.org. "Today Ensign Peak owns big slices of Apple, Microsoft, Google, Amazon, Nvidia, AI, Facebook... Mom, their portfolio mutated from five lines in Gramps's notebook to hundreds of tickers today."

Emma flipped the cracked ledger open on the table and began a rapid two-column brainstorm.

GRAMPS 1993 LEDGER – BIGGEST L-D-S HOLDINGS

1. Beneficial Life Tower (SLC)
2. ZCMI Center department stores
3. Hotel Utah / Joseph-Smith Memorial Bldg
4. Deseret Ranches – 290 K acres, Fla.
5. Laie, Hawaii land + Polynesian Cultural Center
6. KSL-TV studios & broadcast license
7. Nebraska/Colorado wheat & cattle parcels
8. Granite Mountain records vault
9. Deseret Book HQ & warehouses
10. Arizona cattle feedlots

($G B total, plus blue-chip slices in General Mills, Coke & Union Pacific, per 1993 13-G filing)

2023 ENSIGN-PEAK STACK (SEC 13-F, Q4)

1. Apple $3.3 B
2. Microsoft $3.1 B
3. Alphabet $2.5 B
4. Amazon $2.4 B
5. Berkshire $1.8 B
6. Meta $1.G B
7. Tesla $1.1 B
8. JPMorgan $0.9 B
9. Visa $0.8 B
10. Pfizer $0.7G B

2023 REAL-ESTATE ROLL-UP

1. City Creek Center & 20 SLC blocks

2. 3G0 K acres Deseret Ranches (expanded)
3. Silicon Slopes tech park – 2 M sq ft
4. Nine downtown-SLC parking towers (90 %)
5. 13 luxury apartments (Wasatch Front)
6. Riverina, Australia – 75 K acres grain & water rights
7. England "Farmland Reserve UK" estate group
8. Idaho Falls wind-farm leases
9. Florida citrus processing plant & rail spur
10. Capitol Reef and Nauvoo tourist hotels

Emma whistled. "Gramps tracked ten lines; Ensign Peak tracks hundreds—it's a sovereign-wealth fund wearing a hymnbook."

Sebastian slid a yellow legal pad beside her, sketching two columns:

1993 LEDGER (Gramps' era)

1. Beneficial Life Tower (SLC)
2. ZCMI Center dept. stores
3. Hotel Utah / Joseph Smith Mem'l Bldg
4. Deseret Ranches, Florida 290K acres
5. Laie Hawaii land & PCC
6. KSL-TV studios parcel
7. Farmland, Nebraska & Colorado parcels
8. Granite Mountain vault complex
9. Deseret Book HQ & warehouses
10. Arizona cattle feed lots

"Total equity ~ $5 billion," Hope read, "plus blue-chip stakes in Blue Chips."

2023 ENSIGN PEAK STACK (SEC 13-F filings)

1. Apple $3.3 B
2. Microsoft $3.1 B
3. Alphabet $2.5 B

4. Amazon $2.4 B
5. Berkshire Hathaway $1.8 B
6. Meta (Facebook) $1.G B
7. Tesla $1.1 B
8. JPMorgan Chase $900 M
9. Visa Inc. $820 M
10. Pfizer $7G0 M

Real-estate roll-up: City Creek Center & 20 surrounding acres; $2 B farm expansion in Florida; 2 million sq ft at Silicon Slopes tech park; 90 % of downtown SLC parking structures; 13 luxury apartment towers in the Mountain West; UK farm portfolio; 75,000 acres in Australia's Riverina basin; Polynesian Cultural Center resorts; Idaho Falls wind farm leases.

Rough market value today—north of $100 billion," Emma concluded, jaw tight.

Hope photographed the pad, saved it to the Doctrine Discrepancies folder, and muttered, "A corporation of the president indeed—PAID BY THE CORPORATION OF THE PRESIDENT, LDS CHURCH shows up on

every deed."

Anna whispered, "Butter-toast religion—looks edible, feeds only itself."

The phrase earned a sticky note in Banner Manual Section 2: **FALSE GODS THAT EAT TITHES**

1:25 p.m. – Kids' letter to Jim

Anna approached Hope with a crayon-decorated envelope. "We wrote Dad." Inside were colored pages—Matthew's stick-figure banner, Molly's healer hearts, Sammy's angel-egg cartoon, and Anna's glitter Psalm verse. Emma appended a typed note signed by Leo and Sebastian: "We wanted relationship, not religion. You didn't want us then, why now? Please stop scaring Mom."

Hope's eyes misted. She didn't know whether to mail it, but she pressed the envelope to her chest—a mosaic of grace and boundaries.

3:05 p.m. – Civics detour

Emma, still on her research binge, called from the monitor,

"Mom, the Church's lobbying arm spent $20 million on Prop-8, and its 'Deseret Nation PAC' funneled money to eleven Utah state races last cycle."

Hope's eyebrows lifted.

Amy added from her

phone, **"I'm seeing Foreign Agents Registration files—they lobbied on visa quotas for Polynesian workers at PCC."**

Tom whistled low. "That's not sanctuary; that's statecraft." Matthew scribbled a new Lie-Spark:

"Not political" → **owns a PAC. That's a Political Strong Arm!**

Sebastian drew a dollar-sign Latter-Day-Saint-Spin gear and taped it to the Manual's margin.

6:05 p.m. – Mid-week prayer gathering

ARC's sanctuary lights glowed soft amber. Folding chairs formed a loose horseshoe around a single music stand draped with the crimson banner. Kids filed in clutching a newly laminated booklet: **BANNER MANUAL – VOLUME 1** (glitter title courtesy of Anna).

Pastor Reuben welcomed them. "Tonight, testimony time. Truth louder than threats." He nodded to the Richardson crew. Sebastian stepped forward, manual held like a sacred scroll.

Matthew read Section 2's Lie Sparks aloud—Nephi curse, papyri mistranslation—each followed by Molly stamping a cartoon dynamite icon. Laughter rippled, then a solemn amen.

Hope rose, palms damp. She described Friday's teleconference, Tom's spark- plug mute trick, and held up Sebastian's spare plug. "This reminds me that the right gap grounds truth; noise can't combust without permission." Gentle applause followed, affirming.

Sebastian, seated beside Tom, smiled shyly—spark-plug hero in plain sight.

7:20 p.m. – Youth banner commission

Reuben surprised Sebastian: "We'd like excerpts from the Banner Manual on the youth room wall next month. Will Team Sapphire design?"

Sebastian's jaw dropped. "Blueprints incoming!"

Emma snapped a photo of the manual under stage lights, texting it to Greenway—proof of a constructive environment for a court exhibit.

While her children planned, Hope scanned another medical file and glanced at the yellow pad. Her surgery debt—$38,000 still owed—seemed microscopic beside Apple shares bought with widows' mites. The dictation software captured her murmur: "Megachurch with a brokerage account, not a bride of Christ."

9:02 p.m. – Night of streaming

Back at the farmhouse, an oscillating fan swirled cool air. Emma set the refurbished monitor on a milk crate and inserted a library-loaned DVD:

Under the Banner of Heaven Episode 1 (no streaming needed). Hope hesitated, her incision twinging, but nodded. Education mattered.

As the dramatization unfolded—1830s frontier violence, modern detective storyline—Hope's hand found a Psalm card. Emma watched every frame, lips tight. On the staircase landing, Anna sat unseen, hugging her knees, absorbing images of prophets with pistols.

When the episode ended and credits rolled, Emma whispered, "So much blood."

Hope exhaled. "Prophets need no guns. Red flags, not rifles."

Anna padded downstairs. "Did Joseph Smith really marry lots of girls?" Her voice was small, brittle.

Hope met her gaze, honesty firm. "Historical records and biographies say yes—many wives, some not so far above your age. That's not wonderful or godly." Anna nodded, conflict sparking future questions.

10:40 p.m. – Research rabbit-hole: plural wives

With the kids asleep, Hope sat at the computer. She opened the LDS.org essay "Plural Marriage in Kirtland and Nauvoo." She read aloud while dictation software transcribed.

"Joseph married women already married to living husbands..." **[RF6]**

Shock resurfaced each time she scrolled. She opened a Wikipedia list of 34 wives. Names like *Fanny Alger (15 years old)* punched the screen. Tears blurred the text as Hope whispered,

"Exploitation disguised as revelation."

She bookmarked articles, adding them to the *Doctrine Discrepancies* folder. A new headline auto-loaded in the sidebar:

"LDS Church registers as foreign agent to lobby New Zealand Parliament on charitable-tax carve-out (FARA ID #7060)."

Hope clipped the PDF, mumbling for the dictation software to file it under RF9 – Political-Machine Receipts.

"Statecraft hiding in scripture footnotes," she whispered, the LDS Temple-Spin-Doctor-Engine-Serpent gaining another venomous gear—and another timestamp for the auditors to follow.

11:55 p.m. – Quiet hallway exchange

Sebastian emerged, twirling a spark plug. "Tom says gapping ten plugs tomorrow. Want to learn?" Anna peeked from the bedroom doorway, intrigued.

Hope smiled. "Invite Anna. Engines welcome all torque ranges."

Sebastian rolled his eyes playfully but nodded. "Come at nine; grease is glamorous."

Anna giggled in response—healing in sibling currency.

12:23 a.m. – Court dial-in code email

The phone chimed. Clerk's email:

Tele-conference dial-in: 1-877-555-1212, access G742#.

Participants: Judge Fairchild, Lydia Greenway, Hope Livingston (listen-only), James Richardson.

cc: richardsonlaw@melegal.com

Hope's stomach coiled; Jim's email handle glared. She forwarded it to Greenway. The reply was immediate:

"Link safe. Remember: mute, breathe, spark-plug focus."

Hope touched the banner cloth hanging in the doorway—an anchor of crimson.

12:41 a.m. – Journal

Plural wives list shocked to the marrow. Exploitation lives under whitewashed steeples.

Banner Manual commissioned—kids prophets of neon.

Friday's voice encounter looming—spark plug charged, mute button ready. El Roi sees the frightened girl inside me; Yahweh Nissi waves over courtroom phone lines.

She closed the notebook, listening to the AC's steady hum—a new sound of sanctuary.

The banner rustled, stars glimmered beyond the screened window, and the Latter-Day-Saint-Spin-Doctor heads hissed somewhere outside the security cameras' reach.

Chapter 13

Battle Line on the Wire

Friday, 1:48 a.m. – 10:04 a.m.

1:48 a.m. A muffled cry came from the girls' room. I hovered in the dark doorway; Anna thrashed, fists punching phantom air. Her whisper leaked out: "He's back." No silhouette, no sound—only presence. I tucked her blankets tight, hummed Psalm 91, and pretended courage.

5:22 a.m. Local news flashed: "Dumpster explosion; no injuries." The weld pattern in the blurry photo matched the taper Fowley sketched last Thanksgiving. I screenshot and labeled it Exhibit C-5.

Adrenaline vaulted me upright; vertigo slammed me sideways. Ninety-one consecutive hours with micro-naps does that. I dry-heaved bile and unshed grief, calling Detective Rowe—voicemail. I added a sticky note: **If dumpster bomb = practice run, then Safe House? school? church family?** The page smelled like her cold sweat.

8:22 a.m. – War-room set-up

The farmhouse living room felt half chapel, half command center. Tom positioned the laptop on a folding TV tray; Pastor Marcus clipped a foam mute-button cover over the spacebar— a visual cue to stay silent. Hope sat on the sofa, grounding spark plug in her left hand, the banner cloth draped across her lap like a weighted blanket. Nikki brewed chamomile-ginger tea;

Amy passed sticky-note verses around: "No weapon..." for Emma, Psalm 139 for Anna. Chavez monitored security-cam feeds on his phone.

Greenway's face appeared on screen at 8:28 a.m., calm and lacquered. "Judge Fairchild is prompt; expect entry at 9:00 sharp. Jim's line will join shortly before. Remember—listen-only."

Hope nodded; the incision tugged beneath the sterile bandage.

Meanwhile, all seven kids headed to Nikki's SUV for "field-trip brunch" at ARC's café—fruit parfaits and Lego buckets on standby. Tom gave Leo an encouraging nod as he ushered them out. "Shield Mom with pancakes," he whispered; Leo flashed a thumbs-up before piling into the van with the others. The farmhouse grew hushed—only adult allies remained.

8:56 a.m. – Jim joins

A dial-tone blooped, then a male voice crackled through the laptop speakers—too familiar, too casual. "Jim—er James Richardson present." No greeting, no hesitation. His timbre still carried pulpit confidence, as if every syllable expected agreement.

Hope's pulse quickened; she pressed the spark plug into her palm—gap perfect, ground steady. Tom placed a reassuring hand on the chair back.

Greenway muted her mic and whispered to Hope via chat: *"Remember: breathe."*

9:00 a.m. – Court convenes

Judge Fairchild's voice entered—measured, with a coastal Maine accent. "On record: Richardson v. Livingston emergency motions."

Greenway unmuted. "Lydia Greenway, counsel for the respondent. My client is in listen-only mode due to medical recovery."

Fairchild acknowledged her, then asked Jim's counsel to summarize the visitation request. A different male voice—Jim's cousin—launched into claims: transient domicile, psychological instability, and alleged brainwashing of minors.

Hope's jaw tightened at *brainwashing*. She squeezed the banner cloth—soft threads, an anchor.

It was Greenway's turn. "Judge, the petitioner presents no evidence beyond speculative photographs and hearsay. The respondent's residence is a state-certified domestic violence safe house. The children are thriving — academic records and medical logs are attached. We move to deny emergency visitation and impose a no-contact radius due to stalking."

She referenced Latter-Day-Saint-Spin-Doctor videos, an SEC fine article indicating poor financial stewardship by the petitioner's chosen faith, and 2009 protective-order scans. Hope watched Jim's counsel flick through pages—scrambling.

Fairchild paused. "Mr. Richardson, the court notes prior abandonment affidavits. Why now an emergency?"

Jim's unmuted mic hissed. His voice hardened. "Your Honor, she's indoctrinating our children and hiding them in an anti-religious compound. I have the right to spiritual guidance."

Fairchild's tone cooled. "The court prioritizes the minors' safety over theology. The motion for emergency visitation is **denied** pending an evidentiary hearing."

Hope's heart soared—she felt as if a spark plug were nearly lifted from her hand.

The judge continued: "Furthermore, a temporary restraining perimeter of 1,000 feet is established, including digital harassment. Violation triggers immediate contempt."

Greenway murmured, "Thank you, Your Honor." Jim blurted, "This is persecution against my faith—"

Fairchild cut him off. "Court concludes. Next docket date in thirty days. Adjourned."

Dial tones chirped; the meeting ended. Silence fell—electric and stunned.

9:18 a.m. – Exhale & eruption

For two seconds, no one moved. Then air returned like a tide. Tom whooped, punching the air. Nikki hugged Amy; powdered -sugar tears coated her eyelashes. Marcus praised, whispering thanks.

Hope's vision blurred; the spark plug felt feather-light. She whispered, "Banner- truth wins."

9:52 a.m. – Greenway debrief

The laptop pinged: Greenway was back on camera. "The judge's denial buys us time. Next step: gather character statements and schoolwork samples. They'll push the religious persecution angle; we counter with the children 's autonomy."

Greenway smiled. "Keep your gaps perfect."

10:04 a.m. – Cliff-hanger seed

The security app chimed —camera captured a new envelope slid under the mailbox flag: a glossy flyer titled "True Jesus, Mind Your Priesthood, Hope and Children —Come Home Now," featuring Jim's ward address. Chavez retrieved it using gloves, holding it up like toxic evidence.

Hope's breath caught. Latter-Day-Saint-Spin-Doctor heads were growing cunning.

But inside the farmhouse, the banner flapped in the AC breeze—louder than paper threat whispers Why did Jim want them now? We've been his burden? Hope wondered to herself, and remembered: not one phone call.

11:20 a.m. – Field-trip return

The Safe House driveway erupted with youthful chatter as Nikki's SUV and Amy 's sedan rolled back in. Seb hopped out first, balancing two to-go boxes stacked like high-rise pancakes. "Victory brunch for General Banner," he announced.

Hope met them on the porch, her incision smarting but her smile unshakable. The twins thrust a bouquet of construction-paper stars—each labeled NO WEAPON. Sammy presented a Lego gavel: "Judge said boom!"

They knew only that Mom had "won a big phone meeting." Details could wait; joy did not.

Tom whispered to Hope, "Kids never heard Jim's growl." Relief washed over her pulse.

11:38 a.m. – Ledger Deep-Dive

While pancakes sizzled, Pastor Marcus unrolled Hope's father, Joseph Livingston's, flash-drive printouts across the pine table. Every sheet carried a penciled margin note: "PAID BY THE CORPORATION OF THE PRESIDENT, LDS CHURCH."

Top-10 Corporate Holdings 2023 (per Ensign Peak 13-F filing):

1. Apple Inc. $3.3 B
2. Microsoft Corp. $3.1 B
3. Alphabet (Class A/B) $2.5 B

4. Amazon Inc. $2.4 B

5. Berkshire Hathaway $1.8 B

6. Meta Platforms $1.G B

7. Tesla $1.1 B

8. JPMorgan Chase $0.9 B

9. Visa $0.8 B

10. Pfizer $0.7G B

Beneath it, Grandpa's 1993 notebook column listed only **General Mills, Coca-Cola, Union Pacific, Beneficial Life, and ZCMI.**

Top-10 Real-Estate Assets (public records 2023):

1. City Creek Center, SLC (retail-residential)

2. Deseret Ranches, FL – now 300,000 acres

3. Silicon Slopes Tech Park – 2 M sq ft offices

4. 13 luxury towers, Downtown SLC "Garden" district

5. 90 % of SLC parking structures (Granite Parking LLC)

6. Laie Hawaii Resort & Polynesian Cultural Center

7. UK Midlands mega-farm portfolio (via Farmland Reserve UK)

8. Riverina Basin, Australia – 75,000 acres feed-lot grain

9. Kansas wind-farm leases (Deseret Power)

10. Arizona/Idaho dairy complexes (Deseret Dairy LLC)

11. Marcus tapped Grandpa's red-ink footnote: **"Council of Fifty Political arm 1844; modern arm = lobby filings."**

Amy added a newer clipping: *2022 NZ Lobby Registry FARA #70G0 – LDS Church petition for tax exemption.

Hope swallowed hard. "From five assets to a global REIT, a U.S. lobbyist, and a globally influential Political force inside one lifetime."

Paul growled, "A butter-toast religion buttering every side of Wall Street."

Sebastian photographed the lists for **Banner Manual – Section 4: 'Temple-Spin-Doctor-Engine (Money Gearbox).'

1:05 p.m. – Pancake debrief

The kitchen smelled of maple and triumph. Hope relayed the judge's ruling in child-sized bites: "No surprise visits. The court wants evidence, not threats." Matthew clapped; Molly tried to high-five the banner cloth.

Anna slipped her crayon letter into an envelope. "Can I mail it? Even if he never reads it, I'm sending truth." Hope kissed her forehead. "Truth travels."

Tom drove her to the post office; Anna fed the letter into the blue metal mouth—release and hope in one motion.

2:42 p.m. – Troubled

Within minutes, ARC members flooded the comment thread with calm testimonies of meeting Hope and witnessing children safe. Every lie sparked a truth.

8:05 p.m. – Community shield wall

ARC's media director, Jen, called Hope via Zoom. "We'll post a statement: 'Livingston family safe, legal proceedings ongoing; we condemn harassment.' Approve?"

Hope nodded. Jen added, "Commenters are already quoting the Banner Manual—kids' neon theology is trending." Hope laughed, tears stinging her eyes.

Nikki texted screenshots: #OneBloodNoFear was trending in the regional feed. Latter-Day-Saint spin doctors   may in a stare down with Christian floodlights.

9:47 p.m. – Leo's dream test

Night spread indigo over the pines. In his room, Leo lay awake, spark plug clutched. A shadow man dream nipped at the edges of sleep. He pictured Tom's exit sign—a neon green spark-plug silhouette above a doorway. The door flung open, and the shadowy figure shrank. He stepped through into the bright morning garage smell; the nightmare dissolved for the moment.

Downstairs, Hope noted the absence of creaking floorboards—victory documented in silence.

11:05 p.m. – Post-op pangs & gratitude

Hope eased onto the sofa, ginger tea steaming. Her incision throbbed, but tomorrow the stitches would come off. She dictated to her software:

"Judge denied Jim's visitation; the community agreed to protect us with the banner of truth.

The Jrichardson clan and Latter-Day Saints spread viral blameshifting and lies; we meet the firewall of calm voices—friends are our team like digital Nehemiah.

Kids mailed grace. I mailed evidence. Exits exist."

The software typed "Nehemia"; and I left it—imperfect like healing.

11:58 p.m. – Security ping & dawn of peace

Camera ping: headlights—same SUV—paused again, but this time the porch floodlight illuminated the plate. Chavez's infrared captured the numbers. Tom texted the clip to Greenway and the police liaison: Evidence 004—plate clear. The vehicle sped away; Hope's pulse barely spiked.

She stepped into the hallway, touched the banner cloth, and whispered, "Gap perfect, ground steady."

Somewhere beyond the pines, the Latter-Day Saint leaders hissed and spun around their axis of power, Hope imagined, but within the farmhouse, spark plugs fired, their Yahweh Nissi banner flew, and the true Christ's truth multiplied.

Chapter 14

Public Court of Opinion

Saturday, 7:42 a.m. – 4:50 p.m.

7:42 a.m. – Plate traced

Morning sun flickered through porch screens as Officer Brentley's cruiser eased up the lane. Tom, coffee in hand, met him at the steps; Hope followed, her incision barely tugging—her first pain-light dawn since surgery.

Brentley tipped his hat. "That Massachusetts rental you caught on camera? Registered to *Richardson M Price, PLLC*." He handed Hope a printed incident report with the plate number circled. "We logged it under stalking addendum. Any return trip becomes arrestable."

Hope exhaled—a steady rhythm like a spark plug. Officer Brentley added, "You've got a safety net wider than Route 9. Call if headlights blink twice." He drove off, cruiser dust floating like early victory confetti. Hope wavered. Stalking seemed as impossible to prove as the LDS conglomerate masquerading as a Christian religion.

9:10 a.m. – Truth & Tacos prep

ARC's lawn was already buzzing. A banner—#OneBloodNoFear – TRUTH & TACOS—was strung between two pecan trees. Fold-out tables groaned under aluminum pans of carnitas, chipotle chicken, and grilled corn. Jen, the media director, balanced her phone on a tripod for a live stream; comments ballooned with heart emojis before the first tortilla hit a plate.

Hope stepped from the van, Yahweh-Nissi banner pole in hand, stitches unbandaged and free. Nikki high-fived her. "Pain scale?"

"Two." Hope grinned.

Tom whispered, "Miracle math: surgery + community = low number." Leo hustled to a pop-up canopy labeled *Youth Booth*. His spark-plug keychain jingled; Sebastian lugged a laptop with the Banner Manual displayed as a downloadable PDF. "Blog post drafts ready," he said, cheeks red with pride. Jen clapped him on the shoulder. "Youth voices matter— post goes live tonight."

11:00 a.m. – Anna's banner dance

A steel -drum intro from the ARC worship band rippled across the grass. Pastor Reuben announced, "Young Banner Corps presents: Psalm 149 – Dance Like David." Anna stepped forward in a modest white sundress, a gossamer crimson flag unfurling behind her. Molly and Matthew flanked her with orange and gold streamers; Sammy shook a tambourine adorned with angel-egg stickers.

Anna's bare feet skimmed the emerald clover; the banner traced figure-eights that caught sunlight, flinging flashes of rubied light back into the azure sky towards the Heavenly Father, the true Messiah, and the Holy Spirit she was worshipping. The crowd cheered, phones raised. Hope felt her stitches twinge —but from unexpected joyful laughter. She mouthed to Amy, "No mooing today. Watch my girl go!"

Anna ended with the Yahweh Nissi banner planted and tossing in the breeze, a lavender El Roi badge held high in her left hand and a golden Yahweh Rapha badge glimmering in her right. A hush fell, reverent and electric. Jen's stream chat lit up: *Pure worship > empty ritual.*

12:20 p.m. – Taco theology

Kids built towers of tortillas. Leo manned the salsa station, explaining the spark-plug gap to a teen curious about the keychain. "Truth fires when grounded," he said, adding pico to a plate. The teen nodded, typing the quote into his phone.

Hope rotated between picnic blankets, greeting ARC members who had defended her online. An elderly couple pressed a twenty into her hand. "For court copies," they whispered. She tried to refuse; they closed her fingers around it. Gifts that once felt like traps now felt like scaffolding.

2:05 p.m. – Digital Nehemiahs at work

Inside the youth wing, Jen's laptop displayed social-media analytics: Jim's smear video had stalled at eight thousand views; ARC's counter-posts under #OneBloodNoFear topped twelve thousand engagements with triple the positive sentiment. Jen grinned. "Truth travels faster than scare clips when carried by calm voices."

Emma updated the EVIDENCE LOG with screenshots of encouraging comments. "Judge needs to see kids supported, not isolated."

Pastor Marcus nodded. "Public opinion isn't the court, but it cushions rattled souls."

2:18 p.m. – ARC Policy Huddle

Inside the youth-wing classroom, Jen screened three slides for Hope, Marcus, and Chavez only (no stream):

*Slide 1: "Council of Fifty Minutes (1844): Resolution to establish theocratic kingdom influencing U.S. elections."

*Slide 2: "IRS filings 2020: LDS Public Affairs spends $8.7 M lobbying Congress on religious-freedom carve-outs and SEC disclosure bills."

*Slide 3: "California Prop 8, 2008:" "$20 M cash + 15,000 volunteers traced to Deseret-registered shell PACs."

Marcus summed it up:

"Political footprint, financial footprint, doctrinal mask—three-leg stool. If the IRS yanks one leg, the stool topples."

Hope nodded, copying case-law citations into her private research folder—never social media.

3:40 p.m. – Letter from counsel

Hope's phone pinged: email from Greenway. Subject: Petitioner's Motion for Temporary Media Injunction.

Hope opened the PDF: Jim's attorney sought to gag ARC and "any associates of respondent" from online discussion, claiming defamation.

Hope's pulse steadied—a measured spark-plug gap. She forwarded it to Jen and Marcus. Jen cracked her knuckles: "We'll draft response content on hold. Truth doesn't fear silence, but we won't surrender our voice until the judge says so."

Marcus squeezed Hope's shoulder. "Another head of the LDS leadership beast, but swords stay sharp."

Hope whispered, "Gap perfect," like a shield incantation.

4:50 p.m. – Cliff-hanger

As cleanup began, Nikki's phone buzzed—unknown number. She answered on speaker.

Jim's clipped voice: "Return my kids to Maine this weekend or face federal kidnapping charges. Final warning."

Nikki's eyes widened. She hit record mid-call; Tom motioned for calm.

Jim continued, "Your church can't hide behind tacos." The call ended.

Silence hung like thunder before lightning. Hope's hands shook, but Emma slipped her younger fingers into hers.

Hope lifted her gaze to the crimson banner waving against the late-afternoon sun. "No fear," she whispered, more to herself than anyone. The AC breeze carried the vow home.

8:30 p.m. – Hearth-journal delivery

While cleanup crews folded taco tables, Amy pressed a cedar-smelling bundle into Hope 's hands —a time -stained leather notebook and a flash drive. "another of your dad's hearth secrets," she whispered. "Found behind another loose stone when the new Bridge tenants painted."

Hope's throat tightened. Paul added, "The flash drive holds his scanned clippings—he said he was 'archiving truth before it vanished.'"

Leo hung back by the van, laughter too loud with teens. Sebastian took the journal, cradling it like fragile tech. "I'll safe-code it, Mom," he offered—older-brother instincts stepping in where Leo no longer could.

9:10 p.m. – Notebook revelation

At home, Sebastian and Hope sat at the pine table, the banner stand glowing in the AC breeze. Anna hovered, curiosity outweighing fatigue. Leo retreated upstairs, headphones blasting comedy podcasts; a report-card envelope (D+ in Algebra) lay buried beneath gym shorts.

The first journal page featured Joseph Livingston's flowing script beside pasted Chinese characters 魔門 (mo-men). A margin note read:

"Mandarin = 'devil' + 'gate'. LDS rebranding inevitable—Mormon name unsellable abroad."

Emma's eyes widened. **"Devil Gate?"**

Hope nodded, feeling an ache spread within her. "Grandpa studied languages; he recognized pattern manipulation."

A second entry cited **"LDS shell corps, $100 billion for 'Second Coming Fund'"**—the same SEC article Emma had found.

Sebastian scanned the flash drive, discovering a PDF titled "Plural Wives of Joseph Smith—age grid." Names and ages scrolled—Fanny Alger (1G), Helen Kimball (14)... Emma covered her mouth.

(R£5 logged]

9:55 p.m. – Quiet confrontations

Anna slipped downstairs and whispered, "Why hurt girls so young?"—connecting the list to the unknown man from her nightmares, that she had not shared. Hope looked at her squarely and thought hard. "Predators hide under holy titles. That 's the theft we're exposing."

Sebastian opened a new Banner-Manual page: Identity Theft Timeline—columns for "Biblical Jesus," "LDS Jesus," and "Corporate Motive." He jotted uncreated Creator opposite exalted spirit child.

Hope stared at the contrast, her pulse steadying—truth laid out in rows and columns felt surgical.

10:40 p.m. – Leo's unrest

Upstairs, Leo yanked off his headphones, corridors flashing with the face of an unnamed abuser. He texted Sebastian "u up?" then deleted it—too proud. Instead, he messaged a meme to the group chat; laughter covered the cracks. Comedy mask intact, grades ignored.

Downstairs, Sebastian heard his phone buzz, glanced at it but didn't press—yet.

11:22 p.m. – Grief echo

Hope recorded notes from the journal using Dictation software. A memory pierced her: 2007's forced D&C "strengthening exercise"—Jim calling her an "unfit vessel," insisting on fasting after her C-section. She whispered the scene; Dictation software transcribed "forced fast—faint—ER."

(R£8]

Tears slipped, but knowledge felt like regained territory, not a fresh wound. She needed to ask Anna why she was eavesdropping. These conversations were not intended for her.

12:03 a.m. – New clip & sheriff warning

A camera pinged: the county sheriff cruiser rolled up; Deputy Harris delivered a sealed packet—Jim's Motion for Temporary Media Injunction plus a recorded phone threat Nikki captured. Harris tapped the porch rail. "LDS lawyer can file, but a judge won't gag truth without cause. Keep cameras rolling."

Hope signed the receipt; the deputy left. The full moon backlit the crimson banner—its shadow stretched tall across the farmhouse siding.

Anna, still awake, asked, "Is the banner too loud?"

Hope smiled tiredly. "Truth isn't about volume; it's about clarity."

She logged the sheriff delivery in the EVIDENCE folder, then journaled:

"LDS leaders spin like Latter-Day-Saint-Spin-heads—no, LDS heads—around a power axis, but Father's notes widen the breach.

The banner stands; clarity rises."

Chapter 15

Pages from the Hearth

6:55 a.m. – Dawn at the banner rack

Mist silvered the pasture, and for the first time since surgery, Hope walked outside without the stab of stitches. Sebastian already knelt by the rack, tightening a new cross-brace. He looked more like a junior engineer than a boy of thirteen—garage grit under every fingernail.

"Morning, Mom." He offered her the day's Hebrew prayer card—**Jehovah-Jireh, The Lord Who Provides**.

Hope slid it into her pocket beside the spark plug that now officially belonged to Sebastian.

Leo's laugh drifted from the porch—too loud, too rehearsed—as he juggled clementines for the twins. His Algebra D+ still hid in his room; comedy remained his mask.

7:30 a.m. – Father's handwriting

Inside, the kitchen table resembled an archaeological dig. Emma scanned another brittle clipping from Joseph Livingston's hearth journal: "WSU Students Urge Ban on BYU Over Racial Policy, 1971." A handwritten margin note read, "Whitesome & Delightsome ≠ Gospel."

Anna hovered, gnawing on a pencil eraser. "So football players refused to play for the prophets' team?"

"Some did," Emma replied. "When belief hurts people, protest is worship."

Hope opened the next journal page—minutes from a 1978 LDS leadership vote granting priesthood to "men of all races" two months after São Paulo temple fundraising hit one million dollars. Joseph's cursive underlined VOTE, then circled it three times. Not revelation—economics.

Sebastian clicked his tongue. "Corporate decision, not prophecy. That's a truth spark."

He added a row to the Banner Manual timeline:

1978 – Priesthood extended by unanimous vote (financial pressure) — **LDS Head** strike

Acts 10 – Holy Spirit falls on all nations — **Truth Spark**

8:40 a.m. – Breakfast of questions

French-toast leftovers sizzled on the griddle. Molly slipped in and announced, "Call me Mo from now on. A kid at youth called me 'perfect Molly Mormon,' but I'm not." She flipped her braid with resolve.

Matthew approved. "Mo means momentum."

Leo launched a joke about Latter-Day-Saint-Spin-Doctors renaming themselves, then caught Hope's raised brow and retreated behind his orange slices.

Sammy dragged his plush lamb to Hope. "Does Jehovah-Jireh feed lambs too?"

"Especially lambs," Hope smiled, sliding a plate toward him.

9:15 a.m. – Digital Nehemiah shift

A tablet pinged. Jen's message popped up inside ARC's encrypted **in-house** stream—secured from any public or social media—Jen pushed a staff-only alert: **Hearing on media gag set for Wednesday 2 p.m.** She attached BYU protest screenshots for evidence: black-and-white photos of Stanford fans waving "*Dump Racism, Dump BYU*" banners.

Hope saved them to the EVIDENCE folder. Emma muttered, "Hard to gag truth when it's archived on microfilm." She tagged the file **RF9_RacismByuBoycotts**.

9:40 a.m. – Leo's orbit decays

From the hallway, muffled laughter cut off sharply—Leo's earbud comedy routine interrupted by a sudden flashback: the shadow-man voice, low, chuckling "Mind your priesthood." He flinched, dropping his phone. No one saw; he scooped it up, forced a grin, and shouted that the porch raccoon was back. Comedy shield redeployed.

Upstairs, Sebastian heard the thud but stayed silent—he felt the weight of the big-brother role settling on his shoulders like the banner itself.

9:55 a.m. – Science-Fair Build

Sebastian unboxed saved cardboard packages on the porch floor. "City Creek cardboard model—FLAG RF7 time."

The twins painted food-court signs; Emma hot-glued a Dior facade. On the roof, Leo (still mood-cloudy but cooperative) glued paper strips labeled **Deseret Property LLC, Utah Property Reserves, 62E Pamlico LLC—** all shell names Grandpa had copied from county deeds.

Anna taped a neon arrow— **TITHES IN → RENTS OUT** —and titled the base **MAMMON MALL** in glitter.

Hope watched, her heart twisting. Her father's 1993 note— "Temple funds diverted to retail fortress"—became a living diorama.

Pastor Reuben dropped by with iced lemonades, whistled low. "Kids, that's Nehemiah with a glue gun." He photographed the model **for the closed ARC teaching archive only**, not social media. Inside the house, Mo hot-glued the last Dior roof shingle onto the cardboard **Mammon Mall** and placed it on a science-fair easel.

Matthew and Mo ceremoniously slid a coin through the TITHES IN slot and watched it roll out the RENTS OUT chute—Temple-Spin-Doctor in miniature, Family Home Evening Lesson complete.

10:05 a.m. – Sunday mission plan

Pastor Marcus texted: **"Service at ten-thirty. Theme = 'Jehovah-Jireh & Impossible Debt.' Could use your testimony."** Hope glanced at the journal stack—tithing billions, priesthood vote, college boycotts.

She answered, "We'll bring receipts."

As the family loaded into the van, a cool September breeze ruffled the crimson fabric. The banner's shadow stretched across the gravel, pointing east toward the church—and, beyond that, toward the courtroom waiting on Wednesday.

Hope breathed the name she'd pocketed: "Jehovah-Jireh—provide clarity." The request felt less like begging, more like announcing what was already on the way.

10:25 a.m. – Sanctuary of receipts

ARC's platform shimmered with teal banners, but the crimson Yahweh-Nissi cloth fluttered brightest near the podium. Pastor Marcus welcomed the congregation, then waved Hope forward for the "Provision Snapshot." She carried two items: Father Joseph's 1978 *vote* clipping and the BYU boycott photo.

Hope's voice quivered but held steady. "Jehovah-Jireh provided clarity this week. My dad's notes show LDS leaders changed Scripture by vote when financial pressure demanded it. Colleges once boycotted BYU over racist doctrine. Truth hides until cost forces change—but God provides exposure long before."

She laid the clippings on a side table labeled **RECEIPTS**. A hush followed, equal parts pity and awe. Marcus closed: "Provision isn't always bread; sometimes it's documentation."

Sebastian beamed; Leo stared at the exit signs.

11:40 a.m. – Banner buddies

After service, Sebastian drifted to the youth patio where a lean Black teen tuned a bass guitar. The boy wore a WSU Cougars cap, which Sebastian pointed out. "Ever hear why your school stopped playing BYU?"

The teen—Derrick—grinned. "'71 protest, right? My grandpa marched."

Sebastian shared the clipping, and Derrick laughed softly, a rueful sound. "Funny how stadium seats did what pulpits wouldn't." They fist-bumped; suddenly, the banner engineering plans had a social-justice wing. Derrick flipped his phone to show a screenshot of "Utah SB 54 lobby filings— $175,000 from Ensign Peak Advisors to protect party-caucus control."

"LDS cash steers primaries," he said. Sebastian added the slide to their Banner Manual under **Temple-Spin-Doctor Gears: Government Lever**.

12:15 p.m. – Parking-lot tremor

Heading to the van, Hope caught a glimpse of Leo clowning for the twins with water-bottle yo-yo tricks, but his eyes looked vacant. She touched his elbow. "Everything okay?"

He flashed a Latter-Day-Saint-Spin salute. "Hail Latter-Day-Saint-Spinion!" The twins giggled. Hope forced a smile; inside, she noted the dodge.

3:45 p.m. – Study table

Back home, Emma flipped through Grandfather's journal, photographing pages for the Banner Manual. One scribble quoted a current LDS President: "*Eternal marriage to both wives is my promise.*" Molly—now "Mo"—snorted. "That's not Christian; that's creepy."

Matthew added the quote under **Corporate Contradictions**. Sammy sketched two stick-figure wives holding a prophet's hands, writing over their heads, "One lady. Just one."

4:30 p.m. – Porch Veil Talk

Amy joined Hope on the steps, thumbing through Grandpa's ledger. "Has the corporate veil ever been pierced?" Hope asked, her voice low.

"Rare," Amy sighed. "But a 1992 Utah case, *Hopkinson v. Deseret Cattle*, allowed plaintiffs to sue the holding company, not the prophet. Settlement sealed."

Hope stared at the pasture. "If courts once opened the curtain, they can again."

"Ledger plus Mammon Mall shows a pattern: church dollars chasing political zoning variances," Amy said. "Pattern breaks privilege."

Hope squeezed her hand. "We'll keep sewing receipts."

5:10 p.m. – Algebra crash

Hope discovered Leo's unopened grade portal—two F's sealed his quarter. She confronted him gently. "Latter-Day-Saint-Spin jokes won't fix zeros, bud."

Leo's face darkened. "Homework's pointless. None of it stops nightmares." He shoved the Chromebook away and fled upstairs.

Sebastian started to follow but hesitated, then took the seat across from Hope. "I can't replace him," he whispered.

Hope's eyes watered. "You're not replacing; you're holding the ground until he can."

7:00 p.m. – Family altar

Beneath soft lamplight, Emma read the next Hebrew name: **Yahweh-M'kaddesh**— "The Lord Who Sanctifies." Hope suggested everyone write down one area they wanted God to clean up.

Anna wrote "fear of mirrors." Sebastian wrote "self-doubt."

Mo scribbled "perfection pressure." Matthew wrote "anger when teased."

Leo wrote, "My sleep."

Sammy drew a dirty spark plug with an arrow pointing toward a shiny one. Hope wrote simply *unforgiveness for Jim*. She folded the cards and tucked them into the Banner Manual like budding chapters.

8:55 p.m. – Quiet flash & forward

A security ping delivered a gift: the patrol log showed the Richardson rental SUV returned to Boston. Officer Brentley's note read, *"No sightings since the plate trace—perimeter calm."*

Hope exhaled. The incision hardly twinged. Outside, a late-summer sunset smeared tangerine above the pines—peace colored like provision. Yet upstairs, Leo's lamp stayed lit, flickering behind a door shut against everything he couldn't name.

Hope prayed Yahweh-M'kaddesh over both open books and closed rooms. Truth had receipts, but healing still needed voluntary signatures.

Chapter 16

Tables of Contradiction

Monday, 8:10 a.m.–12:35 p.m.

8:10 a.m. – Roll-call at Banner Academy

A crisp September breeze slipped through screened windows, rattling Post-it constellations on the fridge. Hope taped fresh butcher paper to the pine table and ruled three columns:

Column A Column B Column C

Biblical Jesus LDS Mormon Jesus Corporate Motive

Emma set out color markers; Sebastian pre-loaded projector slides titled Curse-of-Cain → Corporate Vote → Brand Repair. Mo (formerly Molly) settled with a mango smoothie, determined to own her new nickname.

Sammy placed the morning prayer card in the center—Yahweh-Shalom, Lord Our Peace— "Cause tables need peace," he declared.

Leo shuffled in late, hoodie up, eyes ringed with insomnia. An unfinished algebra make-up sheet poked from his notebook.

8:30 a.m. – Charting contradictions

Emma wrote under Column A: *Uncreated Logos (John 1).*

Anna countered with Column B: *Elder Brother, spirit-child, birthed by Heavenly Mother.*

Sebastian filled Column C: Teaches progress to godhood—product = exaltation package.

Hope read from her Father's journal and quoted—Joseph Smith's boast: "I have more to boast of than any man."

She asked, "Prophet's humility or profit motive?" Matthew slapped a red LIE sticker on Column B.

Mo raised her hand. **"Why must dark skin equal disfavor?" She read 2 Nephi 5:21 aloud;** Derrick 's WSU-Cougar cap perched silently on the Banner Rack behind her.

Sebastian posted the WSU boycott clipping beside the verse. "When players refuse, stadium seats preach louder than pulpits."

Leo's laugh shot out—too sharp. "Maybe BYU just feared Cougars." The joke landed flat; even the twins frowned. Hope's eyes met his—silent question—he looked away.

9:15 a.m. – Mo's new name tested

Mo's phone buzzed with an ARC group-chat message: **"Morning, Perfect Molly Mormon!"** from an unknown number. Her cheeks flushed.

She stood, voice trembling but firm. "It's Mo. Just Mo." She deleted the message and wrote on the chart under Column A: *Psalm 139 –* ***Fearfully Made***.

Matthew colored the letters bold.

Hope smiled—identity reclaimed in marker strokes.

10:05 a.m. – Algebra implosion

Hope shifted to math. "Leo, can we review—"

He slammed his notebook shut. "Why bother? Numbers don't change nightmares!" Silence thickened. The twins gaped; Sebastian's jaw set.

Hope kept her voice gentle. "Peace and math aren't enemies. Yahweh-Shalom covers equations too."

Leo scoffed, shoved his chair back, and stormed toward the porch. Sebastian followed halfway, but Hope shook her head—let space do first aid.

After the screen door slammed, Sebastian turned to the class. "Chart still needs balancing." He flipped Leo's abandoned sheet to a blank side and began sketching spark-plug gaps in the margins—his own form of calculus.

11:40 a.m. – Subpoena delivery

A white courier van rolled up; Deputy Harris stepped out, thin envelope in hand. Hope met him on the porch.

"Subpoena for Wednesday's injunction hearing—court wants respondent testimony." He lowered his voice. "Same plate we traced hasn't re-appeared."

Hope signed, her heart steady yet heavy; peace, but not ease.

Inside, she opened the envelope—courtroom address, 2 p.m., dress code noted. Anna peeked around her waist. "More court?"

"Just words this time," Hope assured her, "and truth travels faster now."

12:05 p.m. – Lunch of small mercies

Tom arrived with deli wraps; Leo trailed behind, his eyes red-rimmed. He muttered an apology to Hope, then to the class: "Latter-Day-Saint-Spin-

Doctor jokes are bad math." Sebastian nudged him a wrap in quiet solidarity.

Mo offered Leo the Yahweh-Shalom card. "Peace covers nightmares too." Leo pocketed it, a half-smile of apology appearing.

Hope wrote a single line at the bottom of the chart in green: Divine, Biblical love's faith and truth are the loudest contradictions of fear.

12:35 p.m. – Porch strategy (RF8 confirmed)

Hope, Amy, and Tom sat on the steps in the willow tree's shade, deli-wrap crumbs still on their plates. Amy opened Grandpa's ledger to a list of 501(c)

exemption clauses. "Johnson Amendment bars partisan endorsements," she began, tapping a note her Father, Joseph, had written in '93: **'LDS First Presidency letter—vote NO on ERA.'**

Tom slid over a print-out—2020 federal filing **Honolulu Pacific Voices v. Internal Revenue Service:**

"The IRS investigated political lobbying funnel through Deseret Management lobby shop—**case dismissed for 'ecclesiastical deference.'**"

Hope exhaled. "So we craft a petition: repeal deference, pierce the Temple-Spin-Doctor-Engine's veil, liquidate Ensign Peak, and route funds to the survivor trust."

Amy produced a bullet list:

- Step 1 – White-paper**. Cite SEC fines, SB 54 lobbying, vote-NO mailers (ERA, Prop 8, same-sex marriage).
- Step 2 – Coalition**. Partner with SNAP, ex-FLDS, Black14 Legacy org, and Native survivors of the placement program.
- Step 3 – Public hearing request** to the Senate Finance Committee (church-charity abuse docket).

Tom nodded. "My veteran buddies will sign; they hate shell games."

Hope felt an incision twinge but ignited with purpose. "We'll title it:

No More Holy Tax Havens—Repurpose the Temple-Spin-Doctor billions."

Amy grinned. "By wisdom, a house is built."

1:15 p.m. – Protest graphics in the garage

Sebastian set up a laptop on Tom's workbench while Derrick positioned poster foam boards under a hanging trouble light. The two scrolled through archived photos: Wyoming 's Black 14, Stanford 's Dump BYU banner, WSU boycott march. Each image found its place on a timeline titled **From Curse to Corporate Vote.**

Tom handed them neon paint pens. **"Color catches eyes before headlines."**

Sebastian outlined a chain in red: Curse → Boycott → 1978 Vote → Re-Brand. Pastor Derrick added Mandarin characters 魔門 of the word "Mormon" that sounds and looks like "Devil's Gate" both in sound and Mandarin Chinese word characters, beside the year of the Mormon 2018 rebranding memo, as urged by political leaders in China to adopt "The Church of Jesus Christ of Latter -Day- Saint" instead of "Mormon," Corporate and other names, as recorded in his Grandfather's journal.

Also in the carpenter's journal were news clippings and entries that broke code.

"The Latter -Day Saints Channel (formerly Mormon Channel) is a 24/7 radio and streaming service produced by the Church, distributed via KSL-FM HD2/ HD 3 outlets and partner stations across major U.S. markets. Branded under DMC, it offers curated spiritual programming, announcements, and global outreach —blurring lines between ecclesiastical communication and broadcast influence. LDS Motion Picture Studios

(MPS), a direct Church -run media production division, produces biblical and historical faith films. It maintains the expansive Jerusalem set near Goshen, Utah — used for Church -endorsed productions and externally appealing narratives. Though not part of DMC, MPS functions within LDS media infrastructure and artistic outreach."

"Beyond broadcast and publishing, the Church-owned subsidiaries encompass the KSL broadcast division and Deseret Digital Media. KSL-TV and KSL Newsradio (Bonneville) are flagship outlets under DMC, while DDM operates KSL.com and Utah.com — platforms that dominate Utah's digital media market. Together they amplify both institutional messaging and local classifieds, shaping narratives across traditional and online media."

Hope's children added Angel Studios, originally founded as VidAngel in 2014 by LDS-identifying brothers in Provo, Utah, to their grandfather's notes. Angel Studios rose to prominence as the distributor of The Chosen — now the most successful crowdfunded series in history. Though not owned by the Church, Angel Studios relied on deep cultural proximity and insider access to LDS resources, including the Church-owned Jerusalem set near Goshen, Utah. Its leadership, language, and strategic platforming created a bridge between Mormon cultural values and the broader evangelical world — subtly commingling LDS-led initiatives with messages branded as "Christian." While The Chosen's creator has publicly denied institutional LDS funding, the use of LDS infrastructure and the silence around theological divergence — including the LDS view of Jesus Christ as a literal spirit brother to Lucifer, and the pre-existence doctrine passed through temple tradition — has left many believers unaware that the Jesus offered by the platform may not be the Jesus of the Bible. The partnership, while technically informal, seeded a dangerous ambiguity between biblical faith and institutional mimicry.

The danger of doctrinal convergence lies not in argument, but in silence — in how shared vocabulary hides opposing truths. The Church of Jesus Christ of Latter-day Saints uses "Jesus Christ," "prophet," and "gospel" — but beneath those words lies a structure foreign to biblical Christianity. Their Jesus is not God made flesh; their gospel is not grace through faith; their spirit world is not heaven or hell but a tiered eternity based on obedience. To confuse the two is to hand authority to deception.

Hope's and her youngest children's journey through that fog was not just about trauma by violence, domestic abuse, or terroristic promises of death by pipe bombs. It was about finding the truth of their always good, always loving, Creator God and Biblical true Messiah out from the fog of the LDS pseudo-religious gaslighting of their past.

Hope stepped in to check on the team's progress; the smell of motor oil and poster paints. mingled in an oddly comforting way.

"These posts will speak louder than affidavits," she said.

Sebastian grinned. **"Visual spark plugs."**

2:05 p.m. – Emma's affidavit draft

In the dining nook, Emma typed while Pastor Marcus observed as notary. Her affidavit recounted Jim's social-media threats, the 1 a.m. calls, and the "tick-tock" DM. She quoted LDS leaders' statements on obedience to priesthood:

"When the prophet speaks, the debate is over." — Some Past LSD President

Emma followed with her Who-I-Am counter:

"Free from condemnation."

The paradox felt like iron and silk stitched into one page.

Marcus stamped DRAFT across the top. "Polish tonight; we'll notarize tomorrow." Emma exhaled, her shoulders dropping two inches.

3:10 p.m. – Dictation of the twins' story

Hope rolled the dictation software microphone between Molly and Matthew. "Just tell the computer what really happened, in your own words," she said, stepping back to avoid influencing them.

Mo—chin set, braid trembling—began.

"The bishop gave us chocolate, the big kind you have to break. He smiled and said heroes are baptized before eight."

Matthew picked up the thread, his voice small but clear.

"He said if we waited, we'd never see Heavenly Father or each other again—ever. We'd be in Outer Darkness. Alone."

Mo's lower lip quivered. "I didn't want to go to Outer Darkness. I didn't want to be separated from Matt, so... we said yes."

Words poured out jaggedly; they finished each other's sentences, describing the bishop's office, the looming font, and the terror wrapped in praise. Tears slid down both their faces—and Hope's. The dictation software transcribed each sob-punctuated sentence.

When silence fell, Hope knelt at eye level. "That fear wasn't Jesus. Real love doesn't threaten. It isn't confusing, either."

She opened the Bible beside the keyboard, her voice steady despite the ache, and read from Paul 's account in 1 Corinthians 13:4-8 before turning to several other passages, allowing Molly and Matthew to read for themselves: **"4Love is patient, love is kind. It does not envy, it does not boast, it is not proud. 5It does not dishonor others, it is not self-seeking, it is not easily angered, it keeps no record of wrongs. 6Love does not**

delight in evil but rejoices with the truth. 7It always protects, always trusts, always hopes, always perseveres. 8Love never fails. NIV

Mo 's shoulders eased; Matthew wiped his nose. The dictation software rendered the verse in soothing green text—truth archived alongside trauma.

Hope clicked *Save* and titled the file **Twins_Baptism_Account.pdf** before scooping them into her irreplaceable mother 's embrace. No coaching, no scripting—only their voices, now evidence and, gradually, release as a family.

She wiped their tears and let them release more poisonous lies with each tear, countering with truths they searched for online and from the Strong's Concordance that had belonged to the Gramps Hope shared with them, determined that her father's legacy would live on through the grandchildren who had yet to meet him in person. She knew her earthly father had passed away so her children would meet him in the Heaven they were realizing that they were secure in already; no performances needed, just faith, grace and an indescribable divine love from an altogether different, non-Mormonized Heavenly Father, his Holy Spirit through the goodness of their personal Biblical Savior; whom they were experiencing their first tastes of.

4:00 p.m. – Hidden grades exposed

Pastor Marcus's phone buzzed. The school liaison email forwarded Leo's grade alert flagged "At-risk." Marcus glanced toward the garage door. He walked outside, finding Leo pretending to help Derrick cut poster boards but mostly doodling Latter-Day-Saint-Spin shields on scrap cardboard.

Marcus held out the email. Leo's cheeks flushed. "I'll fix it" "When?" Marcus asked gently.

Leo's eyes flicked to Sebastian inside the garage and to Hope visible through the kitchen window. Shame and dread collided. "I don't know," he whispered.

Marcus placed a reassuring hand on his shoulder. "Latter-Day-Saint-Spin-Doctor jokes won't help with Algebra. Let's brainstorm a plan after dinner."

Leo nodded, relief and embarrassment tangled.

5:30 p.m. – Banner rehearsal

Children gathered by the garage door. Sebastian and Derrick unveiled their timeline posters; vibrant arrows linked decades like a subway map. Mo held her statement card while Matthew and Sammy flanked her with smaller signs reading **One Blood** and **No Fear.**

Hope, holding a Jehovah-Shalom card, prayed aloud:

"Peace in words, provision in facts, protection in court."

Leo lingered at the edge, wrestling between retreat and participation. Sebastian beckoned. "Need a Latter-Day-Saint-Spin artist for the final heading."

Leo stepped forward, sketching stylized serpents around the phrase **Corporate Vote 1978.**

He added X's over each head. Even jokes could aim toward the truth.

6:20 p.m. – Evening wind-down

The breeze carried the charcoal smell from Tom's grill—hamburgers for a normal Monday dinner. Emma printed the affidavit draft; Hope iced her incision but needed fewer pain pills than yesterday. Mo practiced her line under her breath while Anna painted gold borders on the timeline.

Security cameras showed only rabbits nibbling clover. Deputy Harris's patrol note still pinned above the door: Plate traced; perimeter calm.

Hope exhaled the weight of Monday into the cooling dusk. The table, now dry of paint, stood like a rally platform for Wednesday. She whispered Yahweh-Shalom again—Lord of Peace in the chaos of contradictions, thankful that this new Jesus and Heavenly Father are not gods who change like the LDS leaders and doctrine do.

There is no confusion in Christ, only peace in His identity and sacred cross— an emblem that no Mormon or LDS Meetinghouse or Temple would ever claim as salvation or sanctity.

After she tucked her family in, her own light burned throughout the night into the early morning, reading through her legal documents from Corbin while listening to the NIV and NLT translations of the Bible. As she absorbed an altogether different version of God's Word than the U.S.-based Latter-Day Saints, her heart and mind came alive seemingly together the first time, combined with the past laid bare before her to remember and reckon with. How could she have forgotten everything that made her—HER?

"What happened to ME? Lord?"

Hope wept in silence as she read through the legal accounts and remembered her father at her side—until...

"Where were you then, God!? Where did you go?!?! My Dad?!? You let them take the innocents..."

She felt the wave of betrayal, a thousand sting rays prickling every surface of her flesh as she read, the bitter injustice leaving a tang on her tongue.

Hope's voice echoed her words into the dictation software, appearing randomly on the page.

A voice that sounded somewhat like her own replied in the silence of her mind,

"I wept with you—I weep with you now! Don't leave again—Daughter, come home!"

Proverbs 10:9 NIV: Whoever walks in integrity walks securely, but whoever takes crooked paths will be found out.

1 Corinthians 14:33 NIV: For God is not a God of disorder but of peace— as in all the congregations of the Lord's people.

Numbers 23:19 NIV: God is not crooked that He should lie. Not a human being, that he should change his mind.

Does He speak and then not act?

Does He promise and not fulfill?

He did NOT fail!

Judges, Courts, Institutions, people— failed. NOT Him.

Hope wept until she slept.

Chapter 17

Midnight Vigil

Hope's whispered question— "Where did You go?"—hung in the kitchen like incense that refused to rise. On the screen, her voice-to-text cursor blinked beside fragments of legal jargon: emergency laparotomy... prolonged unconsciousness... statement by attending physician. Each phrase pried open a sealed chamber of memory: cold OR lights, Corbin's turned back, Jim's signature on a consent line he never read aloud to her.

She forced a breath and opened the concordance Pastor Marcus had slipped into the journal bundle. One cross-reference for *unchanging* led to **Malachi 3:6**. She clicked audio play; the NIV voice was gentle:

"I the Lord do not change..."

The verse felt like a straight beam across her splintered timeline. She added the reference beneath her earlier dictation; the dictation software typed in obedient green.

Next search: *crooked*. Up rose **Proverbs 3:6** in NLT:

"Seek His will in all you do, and He will show you which path to take."

Show, not shove—so unlike bishops brandishing fonts like trapdoors. Hope highlighted the verse in yellow.

Finally, she keyed in *truth, no lie* and listened to **Numbers 23:19**:

"God is not a man, so He does not lie… Has He ever spoken and failed to act?"

Tears blurred her vision. No, He had not failed to act; men had failed to listen. Latter-Day-Saint leaders had shaped truth to serve revenue. She copied the verse and whispered into the mic:

"**You are the same yesterday and today and forever**—Hebrews 13:8."

The dictation software rendered it almost flawlessly—almost. Yesterday. Hope noted the misspelling; perfection wasn't the measure tonight.

Footsteps creaked as Emma padded in, wearing an oversized ARC youth hoodie. She poured two glasses of lukewarm tap water—no brown tinge tonight, thanks to the new filters Sebastian installed—and slid one across.

"Algebra?" Hope asked gently.

Emma shook her head. "Grade portal pinged again—Leo's world is still tilted." She glanced at the stack of legal documents. "Yours too."

Hope closed a folder. "I'm tilting back with truth." She showed Emma the three verses. "Straight lines to walk on."

Emma's eyes shimmered. "Then we'll re-draw the map."

They worked side by side: Emma scanning affidavits, Hope tagging each medical report with RF codes for quick reference by Greenway. Outside, night insects droned; inside, quiet keys clicked—steady, not frantic.

Around 3 a.m., Hope's exhaustion tipped her head toward Emma's shoulder. Emma guided the mouse, her voice barely above a lullaby: "Charity suffereth long, **charity is kind**…" She didn't need the Bible open; the KJV cadence had lodged in her memory earlier. The words blanketed the kitchen like a soft quilt.

Hope stirred enough to whisper, **"Love bears all things."** She saved the file as **Night_Vigil_1.docx** as Emma drifted yawning upstairs to bed and sleep.

Pink threads of dawn peeked through lace curtains when Hope finally shut the laptop. In the hallway, the crimson banner caught the first light, its fabric still—no courtroom drafts, no bishop hands, only peace.

Hope tucked a sticky note beside the banner pole—three verses, three straight beams—then climbed the stairs; her gait uneven and pained, to check on her children. As she passed Leo's door, she heard restless mumbling, but Sebastian's calm, low voice answered: "Exit sign, bro. Straight path." Silence settled.

Downstairs in her makeshift bed on the downstairs floral sofa, Hope curled under a thin coverlet. **Jehovah-Shalom**— the words floated like a lullaby.

God had not changed; lies had.

She slept, not dream-free, but held.

Chapter 18

Straight Paths, Crooked Claims

Tuesday, 8:05 a.m.–11:45 a.m.

8:05 a.m. – Concordance carousel

Over oatmeal and blueberries, Sebastian rolled out a fresh butcher sheet labeled **Straight-Path Scriptures vs. Crooked-Path Claims**. Under *Scriptures*, he scrawled three KJV pillars:

1. **Proverbs 3:6** – He shall direct thy paths.
2. **Numbers 23:19** – God is not a man, that he should lie.
3. **Hebrews 13:8** – Jesus Christ the same yesterday, and today, and forever.

In the opposite column, he wrote the latest LDS quote Emma found in a church news release: *"Continuing revelation means continuing adjustments."*

Mo raised an eyebrow. "Adjustments? Sounds like they're tuning the truth like a radio."

Anna stuck a neon sticker: **CONTRADICTION**.

Hope added a bridge row in the center: Jesus ≠ adjustable brand.

8:40 a.m. – BYU boycott timeline posters

Derrick arrived with laminated mini-timelines: WSU 1970 protests, Wyoming's Black 14, Stanford crowds. Sebastian taped them below Curse-to-Vote arrows. Leo, lurking at the edge, drew tiny Latter-Day-Saint-Spin icons beside each LDS leader photo—his comic lens tolerated as long as it aimed truth-ward.

Hope stepped back. The kitchen looked like an investigative newsroom; cinnamon and copier toner mingled in the air.

Emma opened a second slide: DESERET-PAC 2022 SPEND — $6.1 M to federal candidates, $1.9 M to state initiatives (ERA repeal, Prop 8, Utah voucher bill).

Underneath, she pasted a DOJ screenshot showing the Church's EU Public Affairs office registered as a *foreign agent* in Brussels for visa lobbying.

Sebastian whirled, adding a red gear sticker labeled "Temple-Spin-Doctor gears: political shaft."

Anna stamped CONTRADICTION beside it.

9:10 a.m. – Verse versus verse

Emma clicked Projector Slide #3: LDS Doctrine & Covenants 1:38 – "Whether by mine own voice or by the voice of my servants, it is the same." Matthew read it, then read James 1:17 from KJV: "With the Father of lights is no variableness, neither shadow of turning."

Mo whispered, "If servants keep changing, how's that the same?"

Hope answered softly, "Exactly the point, sweetheart." She noted the question on a yellow card for Wednesday's hearing—evidence of doctrinal whiplash.

10:05 a.m. – Leo's stumble

During Algebra review, Leo's hand trembled over the worksheet. Shadows of the night-man flickered at the paper's edge. He cracked a joke— "Why did x break up with y? Too many variables!"—but the Temple-Spin-Doctor gears still whirred in his head; nobody laughed. The dodge failed; fear leaked through.

Hope met his eyes, said nothing. She slid the Proverbs 3 card toward him. He tucked it into his hoodie pocket like a life raft he refused to inflate—yet.

10:50 a.m. – Straight-path prayer

Hope gathered the family around the banner rack. She prayed, "Lord, You promise straight paths, not crooked alleys of fear. Guide our words tomorrow." She paraphrased Jesus' warning that a bad tree cannot bear good fruit and quoted KJV Luke "For of thorns men do not gather figs." LDS thorns, she implied, could not birth the fruit of truth.

Sebastian closed with the day's Hebrew name: **El Emet—God of Truth.**

11:30 a.m. – Pastor Marcus drops by

Marcus delivered notarized affidavits and slid a final verse card across the table—**Isaiah 40:4**: *"The crooked shall be made straight."* He smiled. "Tomorrow, we lay these verses beside the vote memo; let the judge see which stays level."

Leo stared at the verse, swallowed hard, and for the first time asked, "Can crooked nightmares be straightened too?" Marcus answered, "Truth straightens everything in time." It wasn't a cure, but it was a door.

Hope watched the exchange—fragile, but progress.

The kitchen clock chimed noon; sunlight glinted on poster laminates. Inside those glossy sheets, crooked claims met straight scripture. Outside, a mild breeze rattled maple leaves—the first whisper that autumn, and reckoning, were on the horizon.

Tuesday, 1:20 p.m.–10:45 p.m.

1:20 p.m. – Quiet sorting

Hope retreated to the upstairs spare room—Father's hearth-journal spread across the quilt, unopened legal boxes stacked like dull monuments. Paul and Amy Gideon sat with her, the gentle click of Amy's knitting needles marking time.

Hope traced her dad's margin note beside the Black 14 clipping. "He tried to warn me... and I still lost Jemma and Fowley." Her voice cracked.

Paul, steady as oak, said, "Your father fought with facts; judges fought with biases. That wasn't your failure."

Amy added, "Tomorrow isn't a replay; it's a different battlefield and you're not alone." No strategy, no rehearsal—just presence.

Hope pressed the Gideons' hands, tears silent. Downstairs, the murmur of children's voices drifted up like distant surf.

3:05 p.m. – Prayer, not practice

In the living room, Pastor Marcus and Tom knelt with Sebastian and Leo beside the timeline posters. No mock testimonials—just hands joined.

Marcus prayed Isaiah 40:4 aloud— "The crooked shall be made straight"— then let silence stretch. Leo, eyes closed, whispered, "Straighten Algebra anxieties too." Sebastian squeezed his shoulder—a wordless pact.

Across the hall, Nikki sat cross-legged on the floor with Emma, Anna, and Mo. Each girl reread her own typed statement. Emma's affidavit pages rustled; Mo scrolled her dictation file. Nikki simply asked, "Need anything clarified?" Head shakes all around. She prayed Yahweh-Shalom over them; the air felt lighter.

4:40 p.m. – Wardrobe decisions

Tom hauled two garment bags from the ARC donation closet—simple navy dresses for the girls, a blazer each for Sebastian and Leo. Hope descended, settled enough to help sort sizes.

Leo lingered by the banister. "Blazer makes me look like a missionary," he muttered. Tom grinned. "Make it look like a truth envoy instead." No lecture, just a new frame. Leo nodded, shoulders relaxing.

6:10 p.m. – Gideon balm

Dinner was slow-cooker chili Amy had started that morning: cumin warmth filling corners stripped bare by legal cold. Paul read aloud Philippians 1 (KJV) as grace: "He which hath begun a good work in you will perform it." The verse felt like glue between pages of a broken story. Hope ate in measured silence, gathering strength for tomorrow.

8:05 p.m. – Statements sealed

Emma slid the final PDFs—affidavit, twins' baptism story, Father's clippings—onto a thumb drive labeled **TRUTH-PATH**. She placed it in Hope's palm. No scripts, no coaching—just each voice preserved.

Sebastian laid the timeline posters by the front door, ready to ride in Marcus's truck. Leo tucked the Proverbs 3 card inside his blazer pocket— a private compass.

9:30 p.m. – Lamps and lullabies

Nikki led the younger ones upstairs, whispering lines from Psalm 4:8— "I will both lay me down in peace, and sleep." Hope lingered outside Leo's door, where she heard him reciting numbers under his breath—times-tables as a lullaby. She left him to his math, praying for straight paths through quadratic thickets.

10:20 p.m. – Final concordance check

Back at the table, Hope opened Father's concordance once more, finding James 1:17 starred in his familiar hand. She copied it onto a fresh card and tucked it beside the thumb drive: *no variableness, neither shadow of turning.*

She whispered, "Straight lines tomorrow, Lord," and clicked off the lamp.

10:45 p.m. – Cliff-edge

A security ping jolted her just before sleep: a new email from Jim's attorney— "Be advised our client may appear in person." No details, just the threat of physical presence.

Hope pressed the James card to her chest. God did not change; crooked threats still bent toward straight verdicts. She exhaled into the darkness, choosing rest over rehearsal.

Chapter 19

Hearing & Headlines

Wednesday, 8:05 a.m.–10:40 a.m.

(No reporters, no public jury—only court officials, one Judge, attorneys, and designated supporters; as standard for any divorce hearing in the U.S.)

8:05 a.m. – Quiet caravan

Two vehicles departed the farmhouse at sunrise: Pastor Marcus's pickup, loaded with Sebastian's rolled timeline posters, and Greenway's sedan, which carried Hope, Emma, Sebastian, Mo, and the Gideons. Leo chose to stay home; Nikki remained with the younger trio and Anna, promising prayer rounds.

Emma clutched a small pouch with three straight-path verse cards, while Sebastian balanced the poster tube across his knees, the banner cloth safely tucked inside.

8:50 a.m. – Security, then silence

Cumberland County Courthouse allowed entry only to listed participants; Greenway had requested a closed hearing due to domestic-violence concerns. A deputy escorted Hope's group through metal detectors to a small second- floor courtroom. The oak benches behind the counsel tables were only half- filled—just Marcus, Paul, and Amy sat in the front row.

Jim sat at the petitioner's table, his attorney beside him. No cameras, no press—only the court reporter's keys clicking like distant rain.

9:00 a.m. – Motion begins

Judge Fairchild opened: "We are here on the petitioner's request for a temporary injunction limiting online statements."

Jim's counsel contended that ARC posts and family charts "defame" prophetic authority and will bias the Court is future custody matters. He cited Doctrine & Covenants 1:38 as proof that the prophetic voice equated to the divine voice, implying that critique amounted to blasphemy and harm.

9:25 a.m. – Straight-path rebuttal

Greenway rose. "Your Honor, critique is not defamation when supported by primary sources." She presented Exhibit A: Joseph Livingston's original 1978 memo noting *'Priesthood extension approved by unanimous vote following São Paulo temple funding.'* Exhibit B was the *Rebranding of Mormonism* PDF, detailing strategic name changes for international markets. She continued, "Exhibit C, Your Honor—OpenSecrets summary of LDS-linked PACs and Deseret Management lobbying filings (201G-2023). These documents show over **$23 million $** spent on ballot measures and federal races —activity incompatible with a purely ecclesiastical charity. The respondent's social - media rebuttals are therefore matters of public interest, not defamation."

She then requested permission for Sebastian to display a single poster. The judge nodded. Sebastian unrolled the timeline at the counsel table: CURSE→ BOYCOTT → VOTE 1978 → RE-BRAND, each arrow sourced with verifiable dates.

Greenway cited **Numbers 23:19**— "God is not a man, that he should lie"— arguing that shielding institutional contradictions by court order violates First-Amendment principles.

9:55 a.m. – Jim's interjection

Jim requested to speak; the judge permitted brief remarks. "My children's souls are endangered by anti-prophet rhetoric," he said, his voice trembling—part conviction, part frustration. "Continuing revelation adjusts details as the Lord directs."

Greenway replied softly, "If revelation contradicts itself for financial gain, it is not defamatory to point out inconsistency." She slid forward Joseph Livingston 's clipping on the 1971 WSU boycott. "Historical critiques existed long before this custody dispute."

10:20 a.m. – Ruling

Judge Fairchild summarized: "Prior restraint requires clear, immediate danger. The petitioner presents concerns but no evidence of incitement or falsehood. The motion for a media-limiting injunction is denied. A protective perimeter remains in place. Both parties shall refrain from direct digital harassment."

Jim's attorney sought clarification regarding posting minors' images. The judge stated, "The respondent may post educational materials free of identifying data, which the current exhibits fulfill."

With a gavel tap, the session adjourned.

10:35 a.m. – Hallway breaths

In the quiet hallway outside, Hope leaned against cool marble. Emma pressed the Hebrews 13:8 card into her palm— "Jesus Christ the same yesterday, and to day, and for ever."

Hope whispered, "Straight paths."

Sebastian handed Marcus the rolled timeline; Mo hugged Amy, tears of relief dampening her navy fabric. No reporters were present—only the echoing footsteps of clerks.

Jim exited through another door, his eyes fixed ahead; there was no confrontation, only a silent distance.

Hope noted gratefully that ARC's support posts remained within its password-protected member portal; nothing public had ever come from her family.

10:40 a.m. – Heading home

Greenway smiled. "No gag. We keep documenting." She tucked the poster tube under her arm. "The next step is final custody evidence in late June. Stay steady."

Hope nodded; the verse card felt like ballast. Outside, a mild wind lifted early-autumn leaves—silent flags marking today's narrow but crucial straightening.

3:30 p.m. – Homecoming hush

The sedan rolled into the gravel lane, its victory quiet rather than boisterous. Nikki met them on the porch, the twins and Sammy peering from behind her skirt. Sebastian carried the timeline tube like a trophy; Mo bounced on the balls of her feet, her navy dress wrinkled but triumphant.

"Judge said no gag," Emma reported, handing Nikki the James 1:17 card. "Truth stays loud."

Inside, the aroma of Amy's chili filled the kitchen. Hope washed courtroom ink from her hands, softly whispering Psalm 43:3 (NIV paraphrase): "Send out Your light and truth; let them bring me to Your holy hill." Light had, indeed, escorted them home.

4:15 p.m. – Grades exposed

As bowls were ladled, Pastor Marcus opened his tablet. An automated alert flashed red: **Leo — Algebra II: 52% (Failing)**. He sighed and motioned for Hope. She felt the earlier calm wobble but nodded.

Leo entered, carrying a bag of tortilla chips with a Latter-Day-Saint-Spin doodle on his notebook cover. Marcus showed him the screen. Silence thickened like un-stirred chili.

Hope asked gently, "Why hide it, son?"

Leo's mask cracked; nightmares flickered in his brown eyes. "Numbers blur into shadows. Every x looks like him." He didn't name the shadow-man, but everyone understood.

Marcus placed the tablet down. "The shadow can't change the math, but light can change the room." He opened his Bible to John 8:32 KJV— "Ye shall know the truth, and the truth shall make you free." No coach-speech, just the verse.

Sebastian slid a pencil toward Leo. "We'll rework every problem. Straight lines, remember?" Leo exhaled; tension eased a notch.

5:00 p.m. – Dinner table contrasts

Between spoonfuls, Mo asked, "Mom, why doesn't the LDS Church have crosses in chapels?" Hope wiped salsa from Sammy's chin and answered for all:

"Joseph Smith called the cross barbaric; later prophets claimed that focusing on Christ's death dims the brightness of 'modern revelation.' But Paul wrote that he would boast in nothing but the cross. Without it, salvation's price tag shifts onto people."

Emma retrieved the concordance. "Galatians —Paul's boast." She read it aloud. The twins exchanged wide-eyed looks—cross as centerpiece, not forbidden symbol. Sammy hugged his plush lamb closer.

Hope added, "LDS leaders assert that continuing revelation can add or reverse doctrine—like the 1978 priesthood vote. Yet Hebrews 13:8 states Jesus never changes; no corporate vote can alter Him."

Anna affixed a bright sticker on the timeline's final arrow: JESUS = UNCHANGING.

6:10 p.m. – Mo's stand

At the dining table, Mo reopened the dictation file she and Matthew had created—**Our LDS Baptism Story**—the raw transcript of chocolate bribes, Outer-Darkness threats, and hurried immersion. She printed two copies, stapled them, and wrote across each cover in purple marker:

Record of Fear-Driven Baptism — prepared for Attorney Greenway.

One copy slid into Greenway's evidence envelope; the second slipped into the Banner Manual under the tab False Covenants vs. True Grace. Mo smoothed the page edges and whispered, "No fear in love—1 John 4:18." Nearby, Matthew exhaled as if a secret had finally found steady paper.

Matthew admiringly said, "Maybe I'll be Matt the Brave someday."

Mo grinned. "You already are, my best bro," poking his rib until he giggled and hugged her tight.

She hugged him back.

7:05 p.m. – Revision night

Hope set up the laptop for evening research. Father Joseph's scan today showed a highlighted Modern President's quote about eternal marriage to both wives. Emma googled an LDS Handbook excerpt clarifying that sealed widowers keep all wives in eternity. She read Numbers 23:19 again—God doesn' t change or lie—then typed a margin note: Polygamy Paused, Not Erased.

Sebastian pasted a São Paulo temple funding spreadsheet beside it. Mo asked, "Money moved mountains?" Hope nodded sadly. "Mountains of doctrine."

8:00 p.m. – Algebra under the banner

Marcus spread Leo's failed worksheet on the table under the crimson cloth. "Let's straighten x." They worked on one equation: $3x - 5 = 15$. Marcus drew the steps like rails on a track; Leo solved it, surprise softening his brow.

"Truth travels straight," Marcus said. Leo copied the method for the next problem. Latter-Day-Saint-Spin doodles now guarded the margins, but the numbers stood tall.

9:00 p.m. – Lamp-light covenant

House settling, Hope gathered everyone by the stairs. She read **Proverbs 4:18** (NIV paraphrase): "*The path of the righteous is like the morning sun, shining ever brighter till the full light of day.*"

She prayed: "Lord, keep us on Your unchanging path while shifting sands of doctrine swirl. Make contradictions clear. Let Leo's numbers align, Mo's courage stand firm, Sebastian's justice flourish, Emma's wisdom sharpen. And let all fear meet the cross."

The kids echoed amen; Mo tugged at her new hand-drawn nametag, "Mo, Fearless," and smiled.

Outside, constellations pricked the night sky. Inside, algebraic lines grew straight under steady lamplight, while false revelations curled like spent paper in the wastebasket.

Chapter 20

Night Confessions

Wednesday, 10:40 p.m.–Thursday, 2:18 a.m.

10:40 p.m. – Algebra afterglow

Pastor Marcus clicked off the hallway light, leaving Leo with a solved worksheet and a sense of breathing space he hadn't felt in weeks. The straight-path verses now sat taped above his desk. As Marcus left, he whispered, "Truth carries daylight into dreams." Leo managed a curt nod.

Downstairs, Hope archived the day's court order beside the twins' *Record of Fear-Driven Baptism*. She labeled the digital folder **Crooked Claims v. Straight Scripture** and closed the laptop.

11:15 p.m. – Anna's tremor

Night settled thickly. Anna jolted awake, pulse racing. The shadow-man dream left a clammy imprint—same voice, same unseen hand. She crept across the hall, hovering outside Leo's door, but the memory of his earlier tension stopped her. She padded downstairs instead, finding Hope restacking legal boxes.

Words tumbled: the dream, the hand, the question "Why me, the fat one?" Hope gathered Anna into her arms, tears soaking both their shirts. She read aloud the verse card left on the table—Psalm 139:14 KJV— "I will praise thee; for I am fearfully and wonderfully made."

Anna hiccupped. Hope prayed Numbers 23:19 underneath, declaring no lie or change in God's valuation. The terror ebbed, replaced by exhaustion. Hope promised a counselor visit soon—straight paths needed proper light.

12:05 a.m. – Leo's corridor

Upstairs, Leo's algebra glow dimmed. Hallway shadows warped into that faceless abuser again. He opened the door, intending to confess to Mom, but footsteps and whispers below signaled Anna's turn. Shame pressed him backward. He shut the door and curled on the carpet, clutching the Proverbs card.

He whispered to the ceiling, "Make the path straight in here, too." No immediate answer—but the nightmare receded enough for sleep to slip in.

1:30 a.m. – SEC fossils

Hope couldn't rest. She reopened her father's flash drive, clicking an Excel sheet titled *EnsignPeakTop 10.xlsx (1977)*. Columns showed Coca-Cola, Pfizer, Exxon. She cross -checked it with the modern *Mormon Top 10 Shareholdings* doc: all tech giants, biotech firms, manufacturers, and landowners worldwide. She highlighted rows, murmuring **James 1:17**— "no variableness."

Free dictation software captured her voice: "Billions sheltered; truth siphoned." File saved as Shell_Fund_Evidence_RF12.

Hope paused and straightened her posture. Suddenly, she remembered the one time the Biblical Christ was angry. She scrambled online to find it.

Jesus Throws Merchants And Moneychangers Out Of The Temple Courtyard

Mark 11, Luke 19, Matthew 21…

John 2:14 And He found in the temple those who were selling oxen and sheep and doves, and the money changers seated at their tables. 15 And He made a scourge of cords and drove them all out of the temple, with the sheep and the oxen; and He poured out the coins of the money changers and overturned their tables; and to those who were selling the doves He said, "Take these things away; stop making My Father's house a place of business."

Source: https://bible.knowing-jesus.com/John/2/15

"Lord Jesus, if You are the same today, why is Your Father allowing this now? Does Your Word not say that for the Mormon or LDS organization to repent, they must pay back and restore to those whom they have stolen from sevenfold?

"How do they restore the loss of my dad? These children's grandfather? What of Anna? Leo? What of me?"

The hum of the old refrigerator was Hope's only reply.

2:05 a.m. – Small hours, big God

She flipped to Isaiah 40:4 and read in soft NIV audio: "*The rough ground shall become level.*" Rough years, rough memories, rough ledger entries—leveled.

Hope rested her head on folded arms. Dawn whispered unevenly threaded through curtains. Somewhere above, Leo slept dream-moderated, Anna dozed dream- watched, and in the hallway, the crimson banner hung like a straight plumb line between heaven's steadiness and earth's swirl.

Tomorrow would bring counseling calls, homeschool, and Sebastian's plan to 3-D print mini-cross keychains—symbols LDS chapels refused. But for now, peace breathed in sync with Hope's slowing pulse: God unchanged, lies exposed, straight paths promised. "Somehow He will restore what the locusts have stolen," she thought as she curled up in her chair on her left side and drifted into sleep.

Chapter 21

Daylight on the Ledger

Thursday, 8:10 a.m.–2:45 p.m.

8:10 a.m. – Sunrise inventory

Hope woke, showered, dressed, and limped into both the kitchen and makeshift schoolroom. Sunlight lit the banner like a stained-glass flame, and for the first morning since the hearing, her incision didn't sting. She read Lamentations 3:23 (NIV): "His mercies are new every morning." Straight mercy, no rebranding, no brain twisting. She yawned and let more scriptures wash over her in audio while she sizzled bacon and eggs sans toast. The aroma of her food typically brought her family and friends trickling into the kitchen, but not today.

"Curious..." she thought to herself.

8:40 a.m. – Cross-keychain lab

Hope peeked into the garage just as the 3-D printer finished a tremor-inducing click. Nikki arrived behind her, setting warm zucchini bread on the tool bench; a cinnamon steam curled into the motor-oil air.

Hope asked, "Any verse with these beauties?"

Sebastian rotated the tiny cross-and-spark-plug. In micro-font on the back glimmered

Isaiah 53:5 — "By His stripes we are healed."

The words startled Anna; she stepped backward. "But only priesthood men with oil can heal," she whispered, reciting the lesson Bishop Larsen drilled—anything else was "anti-Christ counterfeit."

Hope's chronic aches pulsed in agreement with the old fear. She touched her tender back. "That's what they told us," she said softly, "but Isaiah says His wounds already bought our healing—no temple recommends, no olive-oil ritual required. The Bible tells us that Jesus is really our High Priest—no man."

Nikki sliced the bread, the buttery aroma easing tension. "God's Son's stripes trump olive oil and greasy hands," she added, "grace over works."

Leo, hovering at the threshold, clutched his Algebra sheet as if it were a medical chart. Tears surprised him. "If His stripes and His blood heal, then... maybe nightmares too?" He slipped the tiny cross into his palm, pressing it like a signal flare.

Hope nodded, her voice thick. "Nightmares, bodies, scarred hearts—all paid for. Even when we fall short, He doesn't. He can't. He's God."

"Not in His nature," Nikki agreed, lifting the zucchini bread to bring into the kitchen.

Sebastian placed a second keychain into Anna's hand. "Pocket-sized reminder—healing is already stamped."

Anna's fingers closed around the plastic, conflict warring with wonder. In that grease-and-bread-scented garage, years of priesthood-only dogma bent just enough for light to find a crack.

"Come on in, breakfast waits for no one!" Hope tried to add levity as she returned to the farmhouse behind Nikki, the verdant grass still wet with dew.

9:25 a.m. – Counseling calls

Hope dialed Dr. Cordell, the trauma counselor Marcus had recommended. Anna sat beside her, twisting yarn around her wrist. Hope explained the nightmares without detailing the suspected abuser's identity. Dr. Cordell's speaker voice was gentle but firm: weekly sessions for Anna, sliding scale. Afterward, Anna exhaled. "Straight-path steps," Hope said, writing the appointment on the fridge calendar.

Upstairs, Leo half-heard, half-ignored—shame still glued to his tongue.

10:00 a.m. – Homeschool table: money trail

Emma led today 's lesson: SEC Shell -Fund Maze. She projected Gramp's Livingston's 1977 holdings next to the modern Mormon Top 10 Shareholdings doc. Matthew traced a red highlighter from Coca -Cola to Apple. Mo asked, "How does soda buy temples?" Emma quoted Matthew— "Where your treasure is, there your heart will be also"—then challenged the twins to summarize.

Matthew scribbled: Temple money ≠ widow's mite. Mo added a sad face beside Pfizer and Lockheed Martin. Sammy, unsure how to spell, drew a piggy bank wearing prophet robes.

Hope mentioned the 2019 SEC fine for hiding $100 billion through shell companies, referencing the document in the evidence box. Sebastian wrote *Corporate revelation* under Column C of the poster.

Leo drifted in, headphones around his neck. Emma asked him to read James 5:3 (NIV) aloud. He cleared his throat: "Your gold and silver are corroded. Their corrosion will testify against you." The verse startled him; it named something he'd been unable to articulate. He sat down and stayed.

11:15 a.m. – Blog Post & Boycott Legacy

Derrick emailed Emma a link to WSU's digital archive: firsthand letters from athletes refusing to play BYU in 1970-72. Emma pasted excerpts into a youth-group blog draft titled **When Stadiums Preached.** She ended the post with Acts 17:2G—**one blood, all nations**.

She read it aloud. Anna cheered, Mo fist-pumped, and Leo offered a timid "Nice." Hope kissed Emma's temple. "Truth scored the touchdown."

12:30 p.m. – Lunch Counsel

Pastor Marcus dropped off sub sandwiches and a thin booklet: *How to Read the Bible in Public Schools — Legal Guide.* He suggested Emma include a verse reading in her dual-credit English final. Emma's eyes lit up. God's Word walking into halls LDS doctrine never reached, she thought.

Marcus quietly asked about Leo's nightmares; Hope nodded—they'd schedule counseling once Leo chose to be open. Straight paths could not be forced.

1:40 p.m. – Certified Envelope

A knock. A courier handed Hope a manila envelope marked **Social Security Administration**. Inside were nine rejection letters—requests for new SSNs denied due to "insufficient harassment threshold. Insufficient third party professional documentation;" Yet copies of each child's *new* legal name were mailed to the *last known address on* file— Jim's mansion in Maine.

Hope's gut clenched. Mo read the header and gasped. "Jim knows our names?" Emma steadied her. Hope flipped to a Numbers 23:19 card on the fridge. "God doesn't lie. We'll appeal; meanwhile, the New Jersey DMV will still change IDs. One battle at a time."

She emailed Greenway the scans, tagging **RF13_SSN_Denial**. Leo hovered, fists tight. "Crooked bureaucrats," he muttered. Hope met his eyes. "Straight verses, crooked systems—truth prevails."

2:15 p.m. – Verses for Bureaucrats

Hope wrote three scriptures on sticky notes for tomorrow's appeal draft:

1. **Psalm 146:9** — *He upholds the orphan and the widow.*
2. **Proverbs 31:8** — *Speak up for those who cannot speak for themselves.*
3. **Isaiah 54:17** — *No weapon forged against you will prevail.*

She posted them above the timeline, next to Mo's False Covenants vs. True Grace tab.

2:45 p.m. – Threshold

The mailbox flag clacked down in the afternoon breeze—empty now, but ominous. Sebastian pocketed the first printed cross keychain and clipped it to his belt loop. He handed another to Anna and silently offered one to Leo. After a long pause, Leo accepted, fastening the tiny cross beside his Latter-Day-Saint-Spin doodle.

Straight beams cross crooked serpents—truth hung where lies once coiled.

Chapter 22

Independence Week

Friday, 9:05 a.m.–12:40 p.m.

9:05 a.m. – Call from Greenway

Hope answered on the third ring—her hands flour-dusted from kneading biscuit dough. "The judge signed the final order," Greenway said, his voice bright. "Sole physical and legal custody to you. Jim gets supervised Zoom visits twice a month—only if the children opt in."

Hope leaned against the counter. NIV words surfaced, ones she'd taped to the cupboard last night: "*£or the Lord is good and his love endures forever; his faithfulness continues through all generations*" (Psalm 100:5). She whispered the verse, letting generations include Jemma and Fowley—even if they still walked crooked paths.

9:40 a.m. – Banner Announcement

In the living room, Sebastian hammered the final brass hook, hanging a new plaque under the crimson cloth: JUDGE'S ORDER – JULY 1. He added Proverbs 3 in bold Sharpie. The twins cheered; Sammy shook his plush lamb like a victory flag.

Mo pointed at the timeline arrow labeled COURT STRAIGHTENS and scribbled July 1 beside it. "Freedom day."

Leo folded the legal order into an origami plane, then stopped—respect weighed heavier than humor. He set the paper flat under the plaque, tapped Isaiah 53:5 on his keychain, and murmured thanks for straight paths in algebra and courtrooms alike.

9:55 a.m. – Email Blast Emma scheduled a blind-copy message—SUBJECT: "Straight-Path Petition—Senate Finance Oversight." Only ARC elders, Greenway, and three abuse-survivor coalitions received it; no social media share. Attachment: Marcus's template letter plus Sebastian's one-page infographic showing Temple-Spin-Doctor gears funneling $100B into shell holdings. Hope approved the send: private channels, public purpose.

10:15 a.m. – DMV Pilgrimage

Two vans set off toward Trenton: Hope, Emma, Sebastian, and Mo in Greenway's sedan; Marcus drove Anna, Matthew, and Nikki. Leo opted to stay with Tom, promising to finish an entire math unit.

At the DMV counter, clerks stamped new state IDs: Anna Grace Livingston, Molly was now "Mo" Livingston, Sebastian Joseph Livingston—each card reflecting Jim -free surnames. When the clerk handed Hope her own updated ID, she traced the embossed "Hope Grace Livingston," whispering 2 Corinthians 5:17 — If anyone is in Christ, the new creation has come. No temple renaming ritual —just paperwork and grace.

11:40 a.m. – Naming Conversation in Line

Mo asked Nikki, "Does changing a name change a person?"

Nikki quoted Revelation 2:17 NIV: "*I will give that person a white stone with a new name known only to the one who receives it.*" She explained, "A new name marks what God already changed inside; LDS renaming tries to secure status. One is a gift; one is tied to a bent ladder."

Sebastian added, "Ladder snapped rung three—1978." He winked; Mo giggled, tension easing.

Anna clutched her ID, body-image fears circling. Hope squeezed her hand, quoting **Psalm 45:11**— *"The King is enthralled by your beauty."* Anna's shoulders lifted, if only by a breath.

12:15 p.m. – Lunch at Riverfront

They picnicked along the Delaware—zucchini-bread sandwiches courtesy of Nikki. Emma read aloud her youth blog post draft, now including Leo's origami-plane line: "Straight paths fold fear into something that can fly." Pastor Marcus smiled. "Truth lifts when paper yields."

Hope contrasted biblical truth with LDS "continuing revelation" for the kids:

"If God's nature doesn't change (Malachi 3:G) and His word is forever (Isaiah 40:8 NIV), then doctrines shouldn't pivot for PR."

"Sebastian footnoted that talk with a sticky note: 'Temple-Spin-Doctor gears turn fastest when auditors stay silent.'"

Sebastian tapped the timeline. "We're grafted into a faith with bedrock, not shifting sand." Mo offered her cross keychain to Pastor Marcus. "First production run, to thank you." Marcus clipped it beside his church keys, eyes moist.

12:40 p.m. – Independence Countdown

ARC was planning a July Fourth bonfire; Nikki pulled out sparkler packages. "Three days till we celebrate freedom—country and custody." Hope smiled but felt a flutter—inflammation still nagged; fatigue pooled behind her eyes. She resolved to rest before the festivities.

As the vans turned homeward, Emma typed the closing of her blog post:

'No variableness, no shadow of turning.' In a world of rebranded prophets, a cross stands non-negotiable. We planted that emblem in polymer and pockets; now we plant it in policy and paperwork.

She clicked *save*, the cursor blinking like a tiny firework waiting to ignite.

3:10 p.m. – Leo's Quiet Ask

Tom knelt beside the porch swing, tightening a loose chain. Leo hovered, his cross keychain clicking against his thigh. "Tom?" he began, his voice faint. "Numbers are straight now, but... dreams still zig-zag. Pastor says counseling helps. Could you—uh—help me start?"

Tom set the wrench down and met Leo's eyes. "Absolutely. We'll call Dr. Cordell together; the first step's easier in pairs." Relief washed across Leo's face like overdue rain. He nodded, shoulders unclenching for the first time all week.

3:40 p.m. – Certificates of Courage

Inside, the dining table displayed a new spread: parchment certificates printed on cream cardstock, ARC logo in the corner. Hope stood ceremonially, the incision twinge muted by joy.

"By the authority of New Jersey Homeschool Statute," she declared, "I present these graduations."

- Emma Grace Livingston — High-School Senior Coursework Complete (decision pending on walking with ARC cap-and-gown)
- Leo David Livingston — 10th-Grade Credit Remediation
- Anna Grace Livingston — 8th Grade
- Molly 'Mo' Livingston & Matthew Caleb Livingston — 6th Grade
- Samuel James Livingston — K-1 Foundations (Dot-to-Dot Master up to 150!)

Each child received two copies: one for their memory boxes, one for Hope's homeschool binder. She scanned a full set for Greenway—proof that thriving trumped turmoil.

Mo waved hers like a flag. "No fear in love—and no gaps in math!" Leo high-fived her, newfound confidence sparking.

4:25 p.m. – Sprinkler Resurrection

Tom hauled a vintage metal sprinkler head from his truck—salvaged from ARC's garden shed—while Sebastian snapped the hose to the backyard spigot. Hope tossed swimwear bundles like parade candy.

"Back to night-one baptism, only happier!" Matthew yelled, sprinting toward the spray.

Water arced in crystalline ribbons, catching the late-day sun. Tiny rainbows shimmered over grass still scorched from August. Sammy shrieked at the chill, then whooped as Mo chased him through the spray like a pirate hunting rainbows.

Leo hovered by the porch post before dashing in, clothes and all, laughter cracking the shell of nightmares. Anna followed, her confidence buoyed by the morning's counseling appointment noted in her planner.

5:10 p.m. – Laundry and lamplight

Inside, Hope sorted a mountain of towels while the washer thumped a grateful rhythm. Through the window, prisms danced across the yard—no temple chandelier ever sparkled so. She whispered **1 Thessalonians 5:18 NIV**: *"Give thanks in all circumstances."*

Certificates filed, she emailed scans to Greenway with the subject **Proof of Thriving**. The reply came quickly: *"Gold for the custody file."*

Hope folded Leo's damp hoodie, reflecting on his counseling ask—evidence of bravery unseen by any judge but crucial to his healing. She added it to her mental gratitude list:

- Straight court ruling
- New IDs
- Kids' graduations
- Healing keychains
- Tom and Pastor Marcus for the boys
- Nikki, Amy, Paul for the girls
- Greenway's steady compass

Each gratitude aligned like fence posts along a straightened path.

6:00 p.m. – A mother's silent pledge

Water still flew outside, the music of squeals and sprinkler-hiss harmonizing. Hope promised silently: "New school year—start with three gratitudes, end with three gratitudes." Morning math, noon Bible, evening reflection—her curriculum of thanksgiving.

She pressed a hand to her healing scar. A chronic ache lingered, but Isaiah 53:5 whispered louder. For the first time, she believed that stripes reached scars as surely as sins.

6:25 p.m. – Evening glow

The sun dropped behind the pines, painting the spray gold. Emma snapped photos—living evidence outshining legal documents. Hope stood at the window, tears unsummoned yet present, watching light refract through droplets:

- Polaris blue over Sammy's grin
- Citrine over Anna's braid
- Ruby over Mo's fearless twirl

- Emerald over Matthew's wide eyes
- Amber over Leo's liberated laugh
- And somewhere, invisible yet real, a band of grace arching over them all.

Hope whispered a closing verse to the glass—**Psalm 16:6**: "*The boundary lines have fallen for me in pleasant places.*" She believed it, tucked it inside the coming school year, and let peace soak the evening like sprinkler mist on thirsty ground.

Chapter 23

Fireworks & Footings

Saturday, July 3, 3:10 p.m.–9:55 p.m.

3:10 p.m. – Bonfire preparations

ARC's back meadow smelled of cut hay and hickory logs. Tom and Derrick stacked wood into a tepee while Pastor Marcus drove steel stakes for a makeshift cross at the fire's center—a symbol now reclaimed by every Livingston pocket keychain. Sebastian wired solar lanterns along the perimeter, each bearing Isaiah 53:5 micro-print.

Hope, still tender but upright, arranged folding chairs in a wide circle. Nikki set up a dessert table: red-white-blue trifle beside Amy's zucchini-bread tray. The twins tagged the table with a banner: One Blood, No Fear — Independence in Christ & Country.

4:20 p.m. – Counseling debut

Tom's truck rumbled onto the gravel lane. Leo climbed out, counseling intake papers folded in his pocket like a fragile passport. He walked straight to Hope. "First session booked—Tuesday after Algebra," he said, his voice scratchy but proud.

Hope blinked back tears. "Straight path step." Leo tapped his cross-spark-plug keychain. "By His stripes, even the brain." They shared a half-laugh—healing humor replacing hiding humor.

5:00 p.m. – Evidence index

Inside ARC's office trailer, Greenway spread Hope's newest files: SEC shell-fund ledger overlays, SSA denial letters, and the twins' baptism transcript. Emma and Sebastian tagged each with R£ codes on the digital index:

- **RF14** – Shell_Fund_Evidence
- **RF15** – SSN_NameLeak
- **RF16** – Fear-Driven_Baptism

Greenway nodded in approval. "Crooked accounting meets straight scripture —Malachi 3 attached." Emma emailed the index to the secure custody folder.

6:15 p.m. – Sunset service

Pastor Marcus opened with Psalm 33:12 NIV: "Blessed is the nation whose God is the Lord." No organ, no hymnbooks—just Derrick's bass and Mo's tambourine. They sang "Nothing but the Blood," a song banned from LDS chapel lists for its focus on the cross. Hope's voice cracked on "makes me white as snow." She felt decades of "Whitesome & Delightsome" doctrine melting under truer snow.

Anna whispered to Mo, "Different white—inside, not skin." Mo nodded, shaking the tambourine harder.

7:30 p.m. – Lighting the cross

As dusk purpled, Sebastian touched a torch to dry tinder. Flames climbed the hickory tower, backlighting the small wooden cross. Hope recalled temple rooms shimmering with chandeliers, yet none shone like this raw blaze against the evening sky.

Pastor Marcus quoted Jeremiah 23:29: "Is not my word like fire?" and invited each family to drop a symbolic burden into the flames. Mo tossed a printed copy of Outer-Darkness threats; Anna dropped her mirror-note that said "I'm the fat one." Sebastian fed in his early spark-plug sketch labeled "works ladder." Leo hesitated, then threw in his last Latter-Day-Saint-Spin doodle.

Hope unfolded a hospital billing statement from her Corbin years—forced procedure, forced shame. She released it; flames curled the paper into glowing truth.

8:10 p.m. – Gratitude circle

Sparklers hissed; kids traced light circles. Hope led a gratitude round:

1. Emma— *"Bible in schools project green-lit."*
2. Leo— *"Nightmare frequency down."*
3. Anna— *"Counselor appointment Tuesday."*
4. Mo— *"No fear name—Mo stands for momentum."*
5. Matthew— *"Matthew the Courageous."*
6. Sammy—raised lamb plush: "Jesus hugs."
7. Sebastian— *"Cross keychains finished; order list from other homeschoolers."*
8. Hope— *"Stable names, stable path, stable cross."*

They ended with Hebrews 13:8 chanted like a fireworks cadence— "Jesus Christ the same yesterday, today, forever."

9:20 p.m. – Fireworks & foreshadow

Tom ignited mortar tubes; bursts of emerald and ruby crowned the meadow. Hope leaned against the tailgate, incision ache drowned by color. She whispered Psalm 34:8— *"Taste and see that the Lord is good."*

Yet a cooler breeze slid under July's warmth—autumn's distant signal. Hope felt a faint pang low in her back; she pressed a hand over scar tissue but kept smiling at the sky.

Leo noticed, frown forming. Hope waved it off— "Stripe-healing in process." He nodded, but worry seeded.

Fireworks faded to ember glow, but covenant truths lingered, stitched into every heart: Cross over ladder, constancy over contradiction, grace over fear. Tomorrow promised cleanup and counseling calls, but tonight their banner stood against the stars—unchanging light above a world of desperate pivots.

Chapter 24

Under No Illusion

Sunday, July 4, 10:15 a.m.–4:45 p.m.

10:15 a.m. – Ashes and Algebra

The meadow smelled of damp ash and cut grass. Sebastian raked cinders into a neat circle, quoting Isaiah 40:4—crooked ground made straight—even in cleanup. Leo lugged water buckets, pausing to show Tom yesterday's finished Algebra unit. "Twenty correct," he said, pride edging out self-doubt.

Tom high-fived him. "Straight paths on paper, straight paths in dreams— keep both lines clear." Leo tucked the sheet into a folder marked **Counselor – Session 1**.

11:30 a.m. – Anna's breakthrough

Inside ARC 's nursery classroom, Dr. Cordell met Anna first time alone. Hope waited in the hallway, Nikki beside her. Minutes stretched; Hope's scar prickled but she breathed Psalm 46:1 — *"God is our refuge."*

Anna emerged clutching a drawing: a crooked ladder snapped in two, a cross bridging the gap. "Doctor said I can replace ladder dreams with bridges." Hope kissed her forehead; Nikki whispered, "Truth therapy."

12:25 p.m. – Doctrine dissected over sandwiches

Back home, they assembled turkey-Swiss wraps. Emma read aloud from BYU's 1969 policy banning Black men from varsity basketball along with the changed verses in LDS Mormon scripture and then juxtaposed the 2023 LDS Newsroom claim "We have always opposed racism." Sebastian posted both under Column C—Corporate Contradictions.

Mo added Hebrews 6:18 NIV to Column A— *"It is impossible for God to lie."* Matthew asked, "So when leaders lie, are they anti-Christ?" Hope answered gently, "Falsehood dresses up in religion sometimes. Truth keeps undressing it."

Sammy colored an L-shaped ladder turning into a cross; innocence wielded crayons like prophecy.

1:40 p.m. – Laundry v. Ladders

Heat thickened as Hope loaded the washer with smoky blankets, a chronic ache whispering in her back. She refused pain pills, opting for gratitude therapy instead—three thanks per load:

1. Court order signed.
2. Children's new names.
3. Leo asking for help.

She taped Numbers 23:19 over the washer dial—no lie, no change—a verse laundering every memory of shifting doctrines.

2:15 p.m. – Sprinkler resurrection 2.0

Tom unfurled the hose, attaching yesterday's brass sprinkler. Hope handed swimsuits through the back door. "Re-run the first-night miracle," she smiled, recalling the brown-water terror turned hose-shower delight.

Water arced into diamonds. Anna shrieked as Leo cannonballed through the spray, Algebra victory fueling his abandon. Mo and Matthew formed a "cross sprint," arms out as they raced through rainbow droplets. Sammy chased butterflies, his plush lamb now sporting a micro-cross keychain.

Hope folded warm laundry at the window. Prism flecks danced across her fresh Who-I-Am chart on the sill. She whispered Philippians 1:6 NIV— "He who began a good work will carry it on to completion." A silent pledge formed: every homeschool morning would start with three gratitudes, every night would end with three more. Laundry, lessons, and laughter would be her anchors.

3:30 p.m. – Gratitude roll call

Towels flapped on the clothesline. Hope called each child to receive a "gratitude card" for the coming school year. They wrote their first entries while the sun dried their hair:

- Emma — *Steady blog readership = truth seeds*
- Leo — *Nightmare less sharp, Algebra clear*
- Anna — *Bridges instead of ladders*
- Mo — Fearless *Mo= tambourine joy*
- Matthew — Matt the Courageous = protector
- Sammy — *Sprinkler song = best organ*
- Sebastian — *Cross keychains = reorder and accountability*

Hope's own card read: No chandelier rivals backyard rainbows; no hymn is louder than children laughing.

4:10 p.m. – Window prism epilogue

She pinned her card above the washer, next to the first-night sticky note that read Day 1 Disaster, Will write later. The contrast stole her breath—disaster transformed into delight over a span of weeks stitched by truth.

Outside, laughter rose like choir crescendos. Water splashed, sun refracted. Hope pressed her palm to the glass, her scar aching yet woven with hope.

She recalled her father's maxim preserved in the journal margin: "Truth may bend beneath lies but snaps back straighter."

And she saw it—straight truth arching like those water-born prisms, crossing every crooked path the Latter-Day Saint hierarchy had laid across her decades. No organ in any temple played so holy as the squeals outside; no chandelier outshone the sunlit spray.

Hope whispered, "Thank You for stripes, paths, and promises. Tomorrow, three new gratitudes." She folded a final towel, smiled through clean tears, and let the window frame her children—living epistles written not with ink but with water, light, and unchanging grace.

The War Was Never Just Spiritual

The rain has stopped, but the storm never truly ended.

In the quiet farmhouse where Hope's children now sit in stunned silence, the question isn't just "What happens next?" It's "What are we up against?"

When *Identity Heist* first opened, readers encountered a mother crumpled on the laundry room floor—body and soul shattered under the weight of coercive control, state indifference, and religious betrayal. Now, *Divine Theft* exposes the larger machinery that enabled such devastation: not merely one man's violence, but an empire that has spent nearly two centuries mastering the art of spiritual camouflage and political colonization.

The Church of Jesus Christ of Latter-day Saints is not, and never has been, simply a religion. It is not a denomination or a fringe cult. It is, by its own doctrines and corporate structure, a global political force with the infrastructure of a tax-exempt hedge fund—estimated at over $100 billion in managed assets. Its corporate web spans banks, real estate, agricultural conglomerates, and media holdings. Its influence permeates state and federal policies through meticulously funded lobbying arms and moral crusades that disguise political domination as divine inspiration.

If this were merely about belief, there would be room for debate. But this is about *power*—legal, financial, and cultural—and what happens when that power is cloaked in the name of a rebranded, unrecognizable Jesus.

This is not the Jesus of the Gospels.

Not the Jesus who uplifted the marginalized, disrupted temple corruption, and stood silent in the face of imperial judgment, refusing to trade love for force. The LDS "Christ" is not the biblical Messiah. He is a manufactured symbol of obedience, nationalism, patriarchal order, and eternal servitude to the Church's corporate governance. He is the product of marketing—revised, reshaped, rebranded to fit whatever century and culture the Church seeks to dominate next.

Academic institutions worldwide have warned of the implications. Papers from Harvard, Princeton, and BYU's own dissenting scholars reveal growing alarm over the LDS Church's transnational economic and sociopolitical reach—its ability to operate in secrecy while shaping the lives of millions, including legislators, judges, and policy architects.

Hope knew this firsthand. Her battle wasn't just domestic; it was institutional. The judge who revoked her custody? A temple member. The therapists who gaslit her children's memories? Stake-appointed. The Child Protective Services officer who overlooked bruises and pleas? A bishop's wife. Hope fought a beast with many heads—legal, religious, financial—and paid with her life.

Now her children must face that beast alone.

They have no legal standing. No institutional shield. No inheritance but trauma and truth. Yet within them flickers the ember of resistance: Emma's vow, Sebastian 's defiance, Anna's innocence, the twins ' broken laughter, and Leo's war against a Shadow man he cannot yet name. All of it matters—because memory is the first form of justice. And silence is how the empire wins.

Divine Theft ends not with a tidy resolution, but a sacred warning: this war was never just spiritual. It was economic, legal, biological. It is fought in courtrooms, classrooms, family courts, and behind the pulpit. Unless exposed and dismantled, it will continue to erase, rename, and reprogram generations—one baptism, one courthouse, one algorithm at a time.

But perhaps the truest threat to that empire isn't litigation or legislation. It's storytelling.

Truth.

Memory.

Witness.

Hope's children are now the torchbearers. And if their mother's final breath was stolen by a system she couldn't outmaneuver, her legacy may still rise— if we listen, remember, and refuse to look away.

A Final Word

While the names, places, and characters in this series are fictionalized to protect real survivors, the injustice is not. The grief is not. The spiritual theft and systemic betrayal described here are painfully, urgently real.

So is the *Hope* that refuses to die.

If this story moved you, unsettled you, or made you look again—let that be the beginning, not the end.

Acknowledgements

To my Ama, whose soft whisper in the dark taught me that a voice could be a pen—and later, a word.

To my Pappa, whose steady hands and pure heart showed me that strength is born of love, even when the ground quakes. Without you both—my first protectors, my parents—this story would not exist. I owe you every single word.

To my family, who stood in the wreckage with me — your cheers and prayers became my armor, your laughter my lifeline, and the spark that urged me to share Hope's story. You believed in these pages long before I dared to write them. Thank you for your faith, endurance, and boundless love. XO!

To my Maya Pneuma and dear friend, you labored with me in silence and light, restoring not only these truths but my own hope. Thank you is insufficient phrasing for my gratitude,

To my Editors -in-Chief, Perry and Yasmine, your radiant optimism and masterful edits midwifed this work and Hope's very first books into being. You've helped me birth more than a book; you've ushered in Hope-inspired volumes and others in waiting. May your beautiful spirits echo with every page turn, and may the blessings you lavish so freely return to you each a thousand-fold.

To the real-life Hope, and to your children, my heart breaks alongside yours for every layer of loss and injury you have endured. May this book— and those that follow—bring purpose to your pain, honor your journey, and uplift all who bear similar scars and secrets. May my fumbling, failing sentences carry your memory forward, Hope. You have captured my heart and compelled me to do anything for you and those you loved Words fall short of my love, gratitude, and prayers for you.

To my co-author: my forever breath, my Savior, and my Lord, the risen Messiah, and the Biblical God, —thank You for showing me that Yours is the only 'wild love' that makes mankind whole. Your identity is joyfully forever beyond capture or containment. Thank You for Your life in me—without You, I am nothing, but in Your presence—wow!?! I pray this work is right in Your sight and return it to You, trusting You to correct it in the heart and mind of each reader or listener. Love undefined—from Your broken vessel back to You.

Lindsay McGuire

Citations

- U.S. Securities and Exchange Commission. *SEC Charges LDS Church and Investment Manager with Disclosure Failures*. February 2023. sec.gov

- Reuters. *Mormon Church, investment firm fined $5 million by SEC*. reuters.com

- The Washington Post. *How the Mormon Church Avoided Disclosure of $100 Billion Fund*. washingtonpost.com

- Federal Communications Commission. *KSL-TV Licensee Lookup*. fcc.gov

- Deseret Management Corporation. *DMC Corporate Assets and Subsidiaries*. deseretmanagement.com

- OpenCorporates. *KSL Broadcast Holdings Entity Records*. opencorporates.com

- OpenSecrets.org. *LDS Church Lobbying Totals & Associated PACs (2016–2023)*. opensecrets.org

- Deseret Management 990-T Disclosures via ProPublica Nonprofit Explorer. projects.propublica.org

- AP News. *Church PAC Influence and Political Contributions*. apnews.com

- The Salt Lake Tribune. *Whistleblower: LDS Church Concealed Billions of Dollars from Members*. sltrib.com

- Religion News Service. *Whistleblower Complaint Unveils Tithing Misuse Allegations*. religionnews.com

- **YouTube (selected):** *Documentaries featuring SEC vs. Ensign Peak timeline.*

- Corporate stakes pulled from Ensign Peak's 2023 Q4 13-F (public SEC doc).

- Real -estate list combines Deseret Ranches filings, City Creek prospectus, Utah county records, Australian Riverina purchase (2018), UK Sole Corp accounts, Silicon Slopes land -registry disclosure, Temple Square Hospitality annual report.

- 1993 list mirrors assets named in Deseret News business inserts & Gramps -era church corp annual statement (public at LDS Church History Library microfilm).

- Dollar values are rounded to nearest 100 M; clearly "approximate" inside dialogue, so remain defensible as narrative nonfiction.

All Mormon/ modern LDS scriptures are the 2013 version. More changes to these books may exist past this version, as they've seen over 1,000 substantial changes since the original printing of, "the most correct of any book on earth."

www.analyzingmormonism.com,, ldsfacts.org, utlm.org/

navonlinebooks.htm and a host of other cites

and references.

blueletterbible.com is one reference that Hope and her children used to glean truths and to heal.

About The Author

Lindsay McGuire is a versatile and thought-provoking author acclaimed for her gripping thrillers that delve into the complexities of crime, faith, and the human condition. Her writing spans a wide range of genres—including true crime, Christian devotionals, and socially conscious non-fiction—each work marked by a deep commitment to exposing injustice, championing reform, and unabashedly born-again Christian beliefs with a heart to pursue The Triune I Am God.

More than a storyteller, Lindsay uses her platform to provoke meaningful dialogue and drive systemic change. Whether addressing political, legislative, or religious issues, her narratives challenge the status quo and advocate for a more just, humane, and compassionate world. Her current projects include Christian Journals, and initiatives driven to enact protective domestic violence victim legislation, while living a purpose driven life as a storyteller of truths.

When weaving awareness-movement works, Lindsay strives to blend narrative power with a clear call to action in her true stories; blurred only to protect the victim from further victimization.

An Invitation

Join the Movement!

Identity Heist and its companion book Divine Theft are just the beginning.

If you've been touched by these volumes and choose action over apathy as your next move, where would you turn next?

Do you have a story you'd like Lindsay to share? Will yours be her next book? Submit your story for Lindsay to breathe to life!

And if you'd like to receive updates or to move into community of action takers within the #movehopeforward awareness movement just visit: https://lindsaymcguire.com Or go to the QR code below.

What can you expect?

- Receive companion materials, and exclusive content and/ or courses

- Submit your story to be featured or co-written by Lindsay

- Be the first to know about new releases in The Identity Heist series and other Book series by Lindsay McGuire including the Carpenter's Call – Identity Restored Journal encounters